# THE GHOSTS OF GLASS LAKE

Landon Wittmer

# 1

"SOME PEOPLE USED TO think crows were rainbow-colored," Mallory said. "Not black."

He and Jane talked while they waited for the others one night a year before Chloe's debut in *Hamlet*. It was late September, but December already stitched the air. They sat at a bench in the center of town, storefronts to their left and the bridge to their right, under which flowed a river feeding into Glass Lake.

"The story goes," he continued, "that the forest animals basically froze in their first winter, so someone had to ask God to do something about it. When no one volunteered, the rainbow crow took off into space to see what he could do."

"And that's where NASA comes from," Jane confirmed. The moon was out, and she imagined a mass of feathers growing distant and disappearing against the glowing portrait.

"And when the crow found God, it told him how bad things were down on Earth, and God rummaged around Heaven and found a flaming stick. The crow took it back with him, but as he was flying, the fire burnt the stick shorter and shorter until it charred his feathers black and turned his voice to, well, crow sounds. And that's how we get fire. And why crows sound like that."

She smiled. "I kinda wish that was true."

"They used to believe it."

"They?"

He took a moment to find the right words. "I guess no one, really. A lot of people think it's a Native American thing, but it turns out it's probably fake. Just a rumor. But it's a pretty convincing fake."

"I guess that makes it everyone's story, right? If nobody's out here saying, 'That crow thing is *mine*.'"

"I guess so," Mallory said, gazing at a starless sky.

## 2

THE MOON ROSE AGAIN over Chloe as she ran through the same part of town the following year. Late autumn cast itself as deep amber in the streetlights she passed. Everything in town was far enough to run to but never far enough for a car. Chloe passed through the sidewalks of the town's center and ran over the short bridge spanning a thin river, an estranged vein of nature in a world of windowsills and welcome signs. Stores here were crafted with short, homely foundations, stuffed together with alleyways connecting city blocks which all funneled to the theater Chloe hurried to. It was a quaint place, she thought, and Jane was waiting for her.

"After the show?" Jane had asked some days prior.

Chloe laughed. "After *my* performance?"

"That's when you're free, right?"

She feigned a pout. "I'll be awfully tired."

"But—"

She wasn't awfully tired at present. She never was after a show. A certain thrill in performance stuck in her bones when she played her part, something that kept her awake at night and awake presently as she rounded the corner. She slung a duffel bag over her shoulder with all the extra clothes worn through the weekend. Now she wore only a thick sweatshirt, a skirt to her knees, and the sun hat Mallory bought her. It was warmer than Opehlia's drag, she thought, and she was glad Ophelia wouldn't keep her up anymore.

The theater stood before her now, bulbs hanging from its awning, the nameplate above reading "The Long Reel" with a list of titles proceeding it. She calmed her pace, caught her breath, and walked into a hall more sanitized and plastic than her stomping grounds at the Vintage—the difference between cinema and stage play. Jane waited inside in shorts and a T-shirt, black hair poking from a bun. She flashed Chloe a pair of ticket stubs as she approached, and when Chloe reached for her wallet, Jane grabbed the arm. "You were *fantastic* tonight," she said. "It's my treat."

"I don't need the money."

She curled a smile. "You got a boy now, yeah?" She held out a ticket. "Hm?"

The events of the past hour flooded her, dragged her eyes low, forced her to silence. She knew things would resolve between them, yes, they had to. But thoughts made her shiver, and an urge bit at her mind to wear Ophelia, to slip into her skin again. She wished she could forget Mallory and fall entirely out of the romance, out of herself, and into lives not her own. As she read her ticket, she wished to be anyone but Chloe Barnett. Ice ossified her limbs, and her body marked foreign lands. She should still be talking to him now, should never have left as she did. But no, they could talk in the morning. She tucked the ticket in her waistband and forced herself out of her head. "Not yet."

"Did something happen?"

"Not quite." She plastered brighter features in her smile. "No. Henry just doesn't think it's for the best yet."

Jane raised an eyebrow. "Dude, we're not kids anymore." She started her way through the theater, Chloe following, around faceless crowds and cardboard cutouts. "How long is your dad gonna treat you like this?"

"I love him." Her voice warbled.

"And Mallory?"

She distracted herself to a dashing cardboard cowboy. "Henry needs me more."

Jane pursed her lips and nodded. "Sorry. I'm sorry. I shouldn't've brought it up."

Henry took interest in his daughter's acting career when she was young, arguing that he picked up on it before she had spoken her first words. He told her she was a natural when she mimed bedtime stories with pillows and blankets, and he told her every week to follow this thing and not to let anything—a crummy job, bad grades, boy trouble, or the monsters out the window—get in her way. Often in the same moment, and much more often in private, Phoebe told her husband he put too much pressure on their daughter, that she was young and trouble would come and that, as long as she grew and lived as Chloe Barnett, mom and dad would keep her safe, regardless of passion. Dad would say he wasn't sure, and that he really did see something in her. But now that mom was gone, Henry's vision became truth, and he bolstered his guidance.

"Focus on your career," he said one night at dinner. Chloe had graduated high school, and two years later, she would meet Jane at the movies. "Make it stable, okay? You'll be happier then."

"I love him, dad." Static ripped the air. An empty chair at the table's head stood between them.

"Have you told him?" Henry took a bite of something Chloe couldn't remember.

"No."

"Wait, please. Okay?"

Chloe sniffed her nose hard to censor any tears.

"If you really love him, won't it feel good to support the both of you? Financially, I mean."

The conversation ended.

"First row or last?" Jane caught her out of a trance. They stood beside the aisles now, and Chloe said first because they always sat in front (Jane always offered the contrary "in case you wanna get wild with it"), though they were used to the others joining them. They took their seats just off to the left.

"Is Pierre coming?" Chloe asked. "Or Cecil?"

She didn't answer until the screen jolted to life, casting the room in shadowed technicolor. "I don't think so. Nope." She collected herself with a breath. "But they loved the show, really. Couldn't stop talking about it."

"I couldn't find them in the crowd, but I imagine that's my fault." She took care to enunciate each syllable's reflection. In every conversation, she rehearsed her stage voice. "It's not good to look around like that when you're performing."

"They were in the back, then."

Chloe cocked her head, and her hat slipped off. "Why didn't they stay after to say hello?" She placed it in her lap.

"I really think you should talk to your dad about Mallory. And Mallory about your dad."

The previews started. Chloe didn't look at her. "I'm sorry?"

"I just"—she dragged on the word—"think you'd be happier. You've been down lately."

"I'm sorry."

"What's wrong?"

Chloe felt small then and wished to be the man swinging swords on the screen, or as the picture changed and Jane waited for an answer, to be the woman hiding in the closet from a stalking shadow. She knew not what was wrong but that Mallory would fix it, but that Henry would fix it, but that she could help her father, and could she ever help Mallory?

"Chloe?"

But she stared into the screen. Jane lolled her head on her friend's shoulder. "He could've come tonight," she whispered. "You would've liked that." She heard Chloe sniff. "He would've liked it too. Is he busy, or?"

"We aren't dating." She fought it back.

"But as friends?"

Chloe's body cracked against Jane as she breathed. "He was busy."

"Okay."

The previews rolled in silence. The movie didn't reach Chloe. With Jane on her shoulder, she felt herself in distant space, alone and cold.


MALLORY FUMBLED WITH THE key (he always fumbled with the key) to the front door. White chalk lines of his younger heights marked the doorframe. He stood twice as tall as the last scratch and wondered how he grew so quickly and felt a quiet dread sweep over him of his new height, new hair, and as he opened the door, his old home.

Mom and dad were at work. The lights were off. It was a large house in the Juniper Heights community. The lawn was cut short and so noxiously green that Mallory thought someone had dyed it, and he didn't understand why there was a gate at the mouth of the neighborhood. Pierre said this was where the rich people lived, but Mallory's parents only told him that they had enough.

Mallory set his backpack down in the kitchen. He turned on the lights, a faint yellow. A note was stuck in the fridge door: *Home at 11. Mac in fridge.* Mom's handwriting. He rubbed his eyes. He pulled out the macaroni and unwrapped its packaging, setting it in the microwave and tossing the note. The slip made him nauseous, and the microwave's buzz only inflamed this brief malady, so he pushed the note under other waste deep in the bin, out of sight. He checked the garage to make certain no one was home, and when he opened the door, a draft of cold air bled inside, and he saw the room was empty, the overhead door closed.

He imagined his parents coming home now, finally while he was awake. Headlights would shine through the windows and the door would slide into the ceiling, and she would park, and the car would warm its small space on the concrete. Mom would walk inside and notice him in the door, ruffle his hair and ask him why he was still awake and shouldn't he be asleep? He smiled at the thought, but the image was only drawn in ghosts, and even in this dream, he couldn't imagine his mother's face or his father's. But the microwave rang, and he hurried to it.

He sat in the dining room with his food and his phone. Behind him lay the hall to the garage; in front, the doorway to the foyer, the living room, the bathroom, the laundry room, and stairs leading up and down to other floors he rarely frequented. He spent most of his time here in the kitchen or in his bedroom.

While he ate, Mallory ruffled through his backpack and pulled out a textbook: *Health and Biology*, required reading for all sixth graders at Highland Winters Middle School. He flipped to his homework and read:

*A strong connection lies in our physical and mental health. If we feel sick, we may also feel sad or inadequate. In shorter bursts of physical harm, like spraining an ankle or biting our lip, we may become angry or annoyed, but as the pain passes, so do these feelings. Similarly, some physical sensations can be tied to emotions. Anger is the brain's emotional response to adrenaline released in the body, which may in turn signal the brain's release of more adrenaline if excitement persists. In rare cases, strong sadness can contribute to physical sickness, as the body shuts off some of its defenses against viruses and bacteria. (NOTE: this rarely causes more than the common cold. Don't be scared if you feel bad after bad news!) Physical, emotional, and mental health should all be noted in our wellness.*

*Some mental illnesses are accompanied by physical symptoms. These often include headaches or migraines, compulsive habits, or "brain fog," the inability to think clearly.*

His thoughts left the page and turned again to his new body. Did he really have too much hair? Sylvia said so, and he loved her, and she loved him too, and he was too edgy about it, and couldn't he take a joke? He thought he could, but with age's fresh affections, did that change? A dark space grew in him now when he thought of Sylvia and holding hands, the same space weighing his teenage changes. He felt a black pit breaking new ground like a sinkhole, caving massive weights on his chest and turning more thoughts to static. He would see her at school tomorrow, and she loved him. But did she worry now about the hole in him, or had she ever concerned herself with it? He shrunk into himself, tightened his joints and pulled his legs to his chest. He felt small, then, as if the world's fringes darkened and he sat alone under the sleepless stars, thinking himself fragile as ocean glass and wishing to turn his skin to it;

to fall, to crack, to leave on a strong bout of wind, to watch the world as a ghost, to watch from mirrors and windows.

Someone knocked. Mallory went to the door and opened it to a boy who hit his growth spurt the year prior, a boy whose tallest chalk line doubled Mallory's.

"What is it?" Mallory said.

"Do you want to go to the lake with us?" Pierre asked.

"Why didn't you text me?"

He shrugged. "Surprise?"

Mallory saw now that Jane stood behind him, and another girl waited in tow. He recognized her from the halls of Highland Winters Middle. She was tall and blond and decidedly not Sylvia.

"Do you have homework still?" Pierre asked.

Mallory clicked on his phone and read the time as seven-thirty. Had he been home for four hours? The sun sank behind distant trees, and Mallory knew that yes, his phone was right, and he had spent four hours thinking at his books and not about them. Four hours of tangling himself in dreams, acting fantasies in his head, and did she really love him? He played the same scene on repeat, each time altering one phrase or movement, but each resulted in her constant, quiet disgust. And maybe she was right, he reasoned. He often felt that disgust in himself when they parted, so it should be right for others to look on him similarly. Pity was a universal emotion. But Pierre didn't pity him, and he didn't think Jane did either. But why didn't Pierre let him know he was coming over? Mallory asked, "Why didn't you text me?"

"If you're busy, that's fine. We just wanna go swimming."

"No, I—" He knew he was busy, that he had been busy since he got home, but he also knew he couldn't help falling into his thoughts and forgetting his work. And now the sun flew just behind the new girl's head and turned her hair to fire, and she wore slacks and a white blouse and Mallory wanted to go with Pierre just for her. So he said, "I'm free" and went to grab his swimsuit, leaving with the others.

Mallory's neighborhood spread on a hill near the middle of town, and a short walk brought him out of tight suburbia to the streets and stocky venues of the quiet downtown. Speakers above the lamps played brassy pop, and everything was tinted with the sun's passing. Around the town was a thick forest, and somewhere inside lay Glass Lake. Pierre's backpack held his and Mallory's swimsuits, and Pierre talked to Jane now about biology. The new girl still glowed, and Mallory turned to her. "What's your name?" he asked. "I've seen you around."

"Chloe." She smiled at him. "And you're Mallory?"

He nodded.

"It's a pleasure." She spoke softly but with a purpose and clarity he didn't expect, the same gravitas Mallory acted with in his dreams. He couldn't find anything to say in return, so she continued, "Have you ever been to the lake before?"

"Last summer." He said, "I mean, we found it—me and Pierre—a few years ago, but we went a lot this summer. What about you?"

She fixed her eyes somewhere in the sky, and Mallory followed the trail and found nothing. But she smiled, so he didn't question it. "Jane keeps asking me to go, but I haven't yet."

"Oh." He tried to laugh. "Did you bring a swimsuit?"

"Under here." She picked at her shirt.

He startled. "Sorry."

"You're dating Sylvia, right?" She cocked her head. "Sylvia Stockton?"

He wasn't prepared for the question and had no time now to ponder it, to mull over if they *were* dating and if she wanted to be and if he wanted to be, and would it be safer to say no? Would word get around faster than he could break it himself, and what would happen if, on breaking it, he needed her back? Regardless, Chloe was quiet—well-spoken, but quiet—and even though he only met her now, Mallory confided in this silence. "Yes and no," he said, and the hole returned and emptied his chest, and with the uncertainty of the relationship in the air, established as a pact with the wind, he panicked.

"Oh. I'm sorry. I think."

"It's okay." He shook his head, but not enough to draw attention. "It's fine."

"Do you believe what they say about the lake?"

Mallory welcomed the change of pace.

They said a lot of things about the lake, *they* being fifth graders and *things* the tales told to scare fourth graders and younger. As a sixth grader, older and with a level of maturity above these gossips, Mallory knew their reports were dramatized. Any ghost story was itself a ghost of nature, leaves rustling, splashes on a quiet midnight, but something inside Mallory always hoped for truth in their folktales, for anything beyond himself and life, some ephemeral meeting with the paranormal to remember, doubt the legitimacy of, and remember again and again, always remembering against reality something above it.

Still other stories spread of murders on the lake's shaded, rocky shores, screams in the night, and still more reports claimed witness to bodies in the water, sallow limbs breaking the surface and drowning back to the lakebed. In response, the younger grades spun their own yarns in lighter tones, and Mallory distinctly recalled playground rumors of a talking fish named Nimbus who controlled the town's weather. A fog of mystery blanketed the lake, and Mallory wondered why so many of these stories were about dead people and why every-one talked about dead people. It returned the hole in him with greater strength than any other thought he could conjure, a vacuum compressing everything inside to the idea of himself starring in a lake story. He was scared not of Glass Lake but its stories. He thought Chloe might be scared of the stories too (why would she ask about them?), but he had to assume she took caution only at swimming and nothing more, and he wanted to comfort her in this, so he said, "No. It's not real."

"The lake?"

"The stories."

"Which ones?"

He pondered this as they neared the woods. "Nimbus and the ghosts. It's stuff kids scare other kids with."

"But people die there?"

He couldn't disprove it. "Maybe once."

"So there could be a ghost."

Mallory stuttered and was quiet.

At length, Chloe spoke under her breath. "I'm not wor-ried. Just curious." She tried to wink but blinked instead.

They stood on the sidewalk at the edge of the woods. Roots cut short at the pavement, and a thin footpath was stamped in the dirt between rising weeds and thick branches. The wall of the forest spread as far as Mallory could see to his left and right, and as Jane led the procession inside in her tall, yellow rain boots, Mallory picked up the rear.

# 3

Jane left Chloe and the theater around midnight, unnerved at how little she lifted her friend's spirits. She knew she was amicable enough and prided herself on the ear she always kept open for her friend, but Chloe had watched the movie silently on Jane's shoulder (and it hurt after a while, but better to endure than object), and at times, Jane thought she had fallen asleep.

She would text her tonight or talk to her tomorrow about it, but she still regretted the sour note she had ended the night with. Jane walked along the edge of the town where across the road, the forest began, seen now in cones of amber lamplight, portholes into a wildfire. She lived far from the Long Reel and farther from the Vintage, the theater Chloe performed at before the movie, in a small apartment overlooking the woods. It was close to what Chloe called the seedy part of town. Jane tried not to think of that place, but whenever she walked home, these scenes fixed themselves in her mind as a tomb in her backyard, and however often she would escape her apartment and walk the brighter sides of town, explore the nooks between ice cream shops and watch the shore of the river turn with foam, a walk home ended every night. But the rent was cheap, and if she capped her thoughts, revulsion went down smoothly. Cecil lived a few doors down too, which did revive the scene at times, and when she was five blocks from home, he stumbled out of the forest and collapsed on the sidewalk across the street. He heaved on his knees in a cone of orange light cutting his upper body from the dark. Jane ran to him.

"Hey," she said, and a small wave of guilt passed through her for not addressing the severity of the situation: Cecil's clothes were torn and muddied—hardly clothes at all—his breathing heavy, palms on the sidewalk. In her younger years, she would've panicked, but now she stood firm. Not firm, she thought, but accustomed. "Relapse?"

He vomited on the roots in the sidewalk and coughed away the bile. Then he darted his eyes around Jane, spinning his head, grabbing it as he spun. "Nobody's here," he said. His voice was vapid, as if he just learned he would someday die. "Nothing here."

"I'm here. It's okay."

"Where did he go? Jane, I'm sorry."

"What happened with Mallory?"

"I'm so sorry."

She crouched down to him and couldn't help but feel she was talking to a child, even though Cecil was some months older than her. He still scanned the world in a frenzy, never landing on Jane. "It's alright. You're safe." But she hadn't seen him worse off before. "We can talk with him tomorrow, and Pierre. It's okay."

"Oh God." He hung on the words.

Jane took pity on him, but she hated taking pity on him. She never found herself caught in addiction, and as she tried to help Cecil in his, she couldn't help but see herself a therapist, someone with authority over the man or boy hunched on the ground. At times in the three years they had known each other, Jane considered distancing herself from him, removing herself from his problems and in so doing, removing the lofty influence she held over him. Then Sylvia left him and her and the others, and his habits grew and commandeered him, no longer Cecil Monroe but a sniffling thing staying out too late and up too long, and Jane couldn't leave, Jane needed to help. "Do you—" she started but thought it better as a statement. "Stay at my place tonight. I'll make room."

He propped against a lamp pole now, and she could see in his eyes, still and blinking, that the stupor was rolling away, or not the stupor but the panic. "Yeah," he said. "I'm sorry."

"What did you do?"

He shrugged, and from the same shrugs in relapses prior, Jane knew he knew very clearly what he did wrong and only troubled about the words to describe it. This insight into his quirks was another pride Jane tried not to take, tried not to use in her analyses.

"I hurt Mallory. I fell in the lake. And I saw faces." The mud had dried, and his hair fell in loose cords around his head. Jane worried about what happened with Mallory, but the lake carried more gravity in his speech, so she asked about the faces.

"Just faces, I don't know." He held his head but spoke firm through thin tears. "I don't know. Like the whole world was watching me, or I was watching them, but everyone in the whole world was people from school." A pause and a cough. "I sank deep. It felt like drowning, and everyone was talking to each other and I watched and it felt like dying."

"But you're okay now?" No answer. She pursued another line. "What were you doing out in the forest?"

He looked at the ground.

"You can tell me if it's Sylvia or her friends," she said. "I won't be mad."

He flinched. Jane caught herself wading into hostile waters.

"I shouldn't've asked."

"I didn't see Chloe, either." He returned to an empty tone, shaking his head. "Her play."

She wrapped her arms around his body caved on the pavement and was brought back to a stormy day in elementary school. It was the day she met Mallory and Pierre, and she had hugged a crumpled Mallory. She recognized even then that girls and boys their age didn't hug—there was no romance in it, but still the notion was abnormal—but it calmed her nerves as she hoped it calmed his. He was crying before she hugged him and he cried after, but she brought him to his feet, so she thought it helped.

Here was another boy who rose from the ground the next moment. Dirt flaked from his clothes. She didn't pry anymore into Cecil's night but led him for the next five blocks to her apartment under the thrumming of night bugs.

It was one in the morning, and Jane couldn't sleep. Cecil crashed on the living room's couch when they arrived, nodding off minutes later, but Jane kept herself up remembering. She played back her meeting with Pierre and Mallory a dozen times, stopping and starting like a faulty film, holes in places of the tape where she couldn't remember faces or settings or words said, holes in her memories forcing her to imagine. She remembered other things too, like sleeping over with Chloe in fourth grade, the zoo field trip, skinny dipping in high school. She didn't think that life was some symbolic thing, a story with motifs and repetition—a sentiment Chloe confided to her and believed—but she noticed themes in her life, as with helping Mallory mirrored in Cecil today, mirrored further in helping Chloe cope at the theater and on the dock two years ago. Failing to help, Jane thought, but trying.

She didn't agree with Chloe about the past fixing a future. The ends of the strings composing her life were tied, and nothing at present stood outside her control. But those like Cecil, she thought, who couldn't handle themselves, diverged from themselves, forgot their history or discarded it—those like him maintained no link to who they were, and this seemed an equal fault as Chloe's.

Jane spent these morning minutes replaying her introduction to Cecil. (Were all the eventful moments in her life introductions?) Sylvia, whose figure smudged in Jane's memory, had invited him to the group's movie night. She took special interest in him, and Jane thought they had something until she stopped texting the group, and Cecil said she was over them, and Jane asked time again afterwards what he meant, but he never answered. Now when she asked, Jane recognized she pried too far.

When Jane met him for the first time at the movies, he was similarly quiet. Shy, maybe, and checking his phone. She didn't expect to make the first move, and maybe it would've been better if she hadn't. It seemed to her that little changed in Cecil over the years she knew him, but maybe she was cynical, and wounds only healed with the hands of a clock.

The digital clock on her nightstand displayed in lumen veins that it was one-thirty now, and Jane stood from bed. She slipped on a pair of dirty jeans and a thick coat. Cecil's body rose and fell on the living room's couch, and a window spanned the far wall from which the descending moon cast itself in silver. She stood by the door a moment, watching the moon and Cecil and thinking what she would do for him when he roused. But he wouldn't for a while, so she slipped on her boots, stepped outside, and climbed down the apartment's stairs.

The air was cold and still, sleeping before a projected storm. Jane walked the same sidewalk she led Cecil down, turning at the path into the mouth of the forest. Some kids would be here smoking, she thought, or worse, but she hadn't been to the lake in a while. She flicked on her phone's flashlight and started in. Thick weeds around the path bit at her ankles, and branches hung low and caught her hair. Middle school symbols and curses etched the bark on passing trees, most of which Jane learned as she aged into high school and beyond, and now a fork broke the path, which reassured her she was still on track. A ten minute walk to the left led to a small field by Mallory and Pierre's apartment, but she turned right and in five minutes stood at the lake.

The beach was small, if it could be called a beach: a slow slant of dirt only a few feet from the water, rocks and roots scattered over the surface. Ghosts of Jane's past flickered on the sand, in the water. There were Pierre's and Mallory's frozen forms as young boys under the shallows. It was the day Mallory met Chloe. Cecil sat alone under one of the beach's trees, watching the breeze cast nascent waves on the water's surface. Glass Lake wasn't especially large, though wide enough to stifle the sound of anyone standing at its antipodes, to turn spectators at opposite ends to vague blots of color, and Cecil looked to the beach opposite him to the town's official boat launch, a slab carved out of the forest where the popular kids and the popular kids' friends and those friends' friends would drink and smoke and exaggerate their body counts. Jane couldn't make out any boats there now, but Cecil stared. On this side of the lake lay a thin wooden dock missing a few of its boards and losing more each month, and Chloe rested at its end, her feet dangling in the lake. She looked into the water, and Jane remembered the feel of her frozen skin. She had asked Jane how many people drown each year, and how many of those drownings were planned. Jane didn't have an answer and regretted not looking it up then, though a statistic probably wouldn't have helped. In Jane's mind, Chloe still crumbled into her from the movie hours prior. Was grief a theme so invoked in her that it bled into Jane?

Jane had little to lose but her friends, but dread gnawed at her that she would wake one day and forget everything she was and everything she had. Irrational, but she believed it could happen, maybe that it would happen, and she prematurely grieved a world without memories or history. Chloe lived forever inside the loss of her mother, but could she wake one day ignorant of those moments, and would she be happy then?

A small fishing boat hid in the moon's reflection in the middle of the lake. Jane caught its contours in the dark and recalled the same boat buried upright in the dirt beside her for years. Like the dock, it was a weathered thing, likely a few boards loose and ready to capsize. But in her elementary years, before the boat was beached (likely a high schooler's prank, Jane thought at the time. Now she imagined someone with authority viewed it a safety hazard—which, in fairness, she couldn't argue against—and had it scuttled), she carried herself with a pirate's air, ruling the lake with Mallory and Pierre. The skiff had a sail then, something lost in its funeral. She didn't know how or why it was in the water now, who or what moved it from grave to sea, but compulsion gripped her to swim to the vessel and drag it back to shore and cement it in her mind and in the dirt again, to return something, to create permanence. If it would be gone by tomorrow, Jane wished once more to adjust the mast and run her hand along the rail, to patch the holes if she could, but more, to stay with it before it left at last. She wished to stay forever with the boat and watch the ghosts—herself and the others, images of themselves as children again—run in its shell or stand on the beach and watch it from a distance, under the moonlight, and maybe the others could come and see it off.

The ghosts were watching it too now, Mallory, Pierre, Cecil, and Chloe. The boat swayed in broken light, and as it foundered and fell to its bed, the ghosts followed, and the lake breathed over and sealed the disturbance the sinking thing made.

# 4

IN THIRD GRADE, JANE thought she would never age. Or maybe she would, but she had no reference but her mother for what her older self would look like, and Jane didn't think her mom was very pretty, so when she imagined herself ten years from then, in her mind's eye stood only a taller Jane, as if she were stretched in a carnival mirror. She would certainly feel the same as she did now and maintain her love of animals and cartoons. Life in third grade was a calendar of recess and homework only, and she reasoned that when she grew up, extra time for recess and homework would abound, and she would still talk to the fish. Leaves would always be green for her, and regardless of the weather, she always wore rain boots because they made her jump higher.

It stormed one day at school. She was wrestling an alligator at recess when it happened. The weekend prior, she had watched nature documentaries with her dad, and this struck her:

"What's that one?" she asked as long, gray spikes passed the bottom of the screen.

"That's a"—he waited for the narrator—"'caiman?' It's a crocodile."

"Where does he live?"

"Near water," he said. "Where it's hot."

"Woah." For the next hour, these reptiles slunk through the scene, and Jane was enthralled. She hid when they took their prey and cooed as their eggs hatched; they were her favorites.

She wrestled the alligator in the playground next to the swings (he was scaring her friends—it was only natural). It was certainly an imaginary beast (and imaginary friends), but it was a fight nonetheless, and with the same bravado she saw the man on TV flip a crocodile, Jane stamped her boots in the ground and spun the lizard to its back. She raised her fists in triumph.

With a thundercrack, the rain hit.

The alligator righted himself, put on his cool sunglasses, and told Jane he'd see her tomorrow. He scuttled back toward the woods, maybe to smoke cigarettes with Nimbus, but the rain swallowed him after a few steps, vanishing. Chloe had seen Ms. Lizzie and Mr. Smith smoking cigarettes too. She thought it made them look like teapots.

The storm air was gray with fog, patches of muddied light seeping in from far away, and the sky was tinted a wan green. The playground full of laughing, crying, screaming kids, went quiet a moment as lightning ripped the air, resuming louder as the flood fell. It would be the greatest storm any of them would live through. Parents told their children that morning, patting them down with coats and gloves, that a shower was coming, and the children spread rumors of a hurricane to batter and break the school's windows. Whatever it was, it mixed and matted Jane's hair. Drops pelted her arms like loose dodgeballs, though they hit so often that it stopped hurting and became a steady weight in her clothes, like gravity had only now switched on. She drudged to the big, plastic castle, refuging under one of its slides. The kids were louder now and all around her, and she couldn't tell if they were happy or scared. Jane wasn't scared, and she told herself she wasn't scared, but everyone was so loud, and the rain built like static in her ears, so in any case, she wasn't happy.

Then a light blipped through the storm's gray curtain. More lights joined it, and with them came voices.

"Kids!" they said. "Come on in."

And then "Indoor recess!"

Jane was the first to rush forward, or she thought she was, but no one else stood close enough for her to see. She met a light at its source where her math teacher stood under an umbrella, herding the kids inside. "Hello, Jane!" she said with a voice much higher than normal. Jane smiled and nodded.

The other kids stamped from behind as a pack of buffalo, and Jane trailed them inside. The teacher moved on, and Jane heard her scold, "Come on, Pierre, let's go. No splashing."

Lockers hugged tight in the halls, each with a name tag and crayon portrait. The carpet had stiffened over the years, and everywhere smelled like apples and hand sanitizer. Jane was herded into Ms. Lizzie's homeroom, squeezing through the bottleneck at the door, finding her place at the fish tank. She didn't trouble herself much with toys, and maybe her friends would feel better now that she was soaked like them. The guy from the animal show said fish always loved friends. Maybe they knew her name now.

"Hi guys. It's Jane."

Nothing. But they glubbed their mouths, and that was a start. She had a conversation with the fish.

Ms. Lizzie dragged Pierre, drenched and sagging like a willow tree, by his shirt sleeve. She tried to dry him with toilet paper, but fresh puddles soaked the floor where his feet stomped. He always stomped, Jane noticed, like the steps of the tyrannosaurus he dawdled over. Pierre was on the taller side, his hair buzzed short, a shirt full of movie characters. He scuttled next to Mallory, a shorter boy with hair to his cheeks, a dress shirt. Mallory didn't move away but placed his book of dinosaurs between them.

"The ste-go-saurus is my favorite."

"He goes *agh*!" Pierre punched the ground and water sprinkled the page that Mallory frantically dried with his shirt sleeve.

"He has a big tail that smashes things."

Jane was still talking with the fish. "Can you live in the rain?" she asked. Her eyes grew wide. "Could you *fly?*"

"That is for the flying fish," the Tetra said. He sounded like an aristocrat because Jane believed all tetras were fancy. "We much prefer the rivers. And lakes."

She knew a lot about flying fish, just as she knew a lot about every animal. "Do you know any flying fish?" she asked.

"Oh, they're all above you. Look in the clouds!"

Jane giggled because even birds didn't go that high. But Ms. Lizzie said clouds were made of water, so why couldn't fish live there? She was asking the tetra more about his cousins in the clouds, but her speech drifted with her attention behind her.

"I like the, the please-ee-o-saurus," Pierre said. "He's like a big shark or a dolphin and he gets all wet."

Mallory looked at him, and they laughed.

"He lives in the water, though," he said to conclude any inquiry into the beast. But when the words left his mouth, a gleam lit both their eyes. "Outside," Pierre whispered, and, checking that some other rascal student occupied the teacher, the two snuck to the hall. Jane wanted to see a dinosaur too, so she followed at a distance.

They raced in the hall, taking a sharp left to the recess door, raising their hands to open it. It wasn't locked. A gust of frozen air broke into the hallway as the door folded open. The world outside looked as if night had risen early, and rain still came as a torrent only sparsely visible from inside. Pierre broke the threshold first, running into the dark well, lost. Mallory hesitated at the door, sticking his hand out and taking it back, but Pierre laughed somewhere far off, and Mallory stepped through the threshold. Jane watched this from around the corner, and as Mallory vanished in the storm, she chased after.

Inside, the storm had sounded a low crackle on the roof, like the garbage truck scraping against the sidewalk before school. Outside now, it was a war fought with firecrackers popping on the playground's spongy turf, and it hurt Jane's skin if she stopped moving too long. She looked for the others in vain, and she couldn't see the playground equipment either, and she didn't know where she was. It was the same loose blindness she felt as she navigated her house at night, all the walls and stairs newly foreign.

"Please-ee-o-saaaaur," Pierre called around her, "where are you?"

"It's cold out here," Mallory said. Was he behind her?

She ran forward to where the swings should be, and Pierre was there, spinning in circles. In middle school, she would question him as to why he twirled then, and he would tell her, "If you want to find something, you have to look where you haven't looked. That was just *efficient*." He stalled now, dizzy and stupefied in a world he, like Jane, didn't recognize. Mallory said something close, and he turned to it.

"Please-ee-o-saur!" He pointed at a figure in the mist.

"I'm Jane." She stepped clear into view. "I wanna find one too."

"Mallory, it's him!"

"I'm not a please-o-saur!"

Behind them: "Can we go back?"

Pierre challenged her. "What's your name, dinosaur?"

"I said 'Jane.'"

"I'm scared."

"That's not a dinosaur name."

"What's a dinosaur name?"

"Guys." His voice warbled. "Guys?"

Pierre was stumped. "I guess I think we need to find one first."

She agreed to help him in the hunt, and they moved as a unit so as not to lose each other because Pierre said that's when he attacks. In practice, they lost each other within a few steps, and Pierre thought he saw something move and sped forward without warning. Jane called for him, but he was lost in the hunt. She was alone.

Wandering, she found small pleasures in the rain. It pained and chilled her skin, but it was quiet. Well, it wasn't quiet either, but was like the fan she turned on to fall asleep to, making everything else quiet. She could only see a few feet around her, which meant nothing lived past that border. She could only worry about herself and maybe a stray please-ee-o-saur. The space fostered her mind, and as she looked up, wonderful fish flew by on their commutes.

She lived in nothing—numb skin, blind sight—but she could think anything, and in the senses' torpor, she could be whoever she wanted to be. To be Rachel with all her friends or Pierre with his dinosaur books, but always keeping her name, just improving on it. She was fond of the rain from then on, and whenever a storm brewed after, she would imagine herself a romantic, would imagine herself so much more than Jane Clerval.

Then she heard it. The please-ee-o-saur moaned somewhere close to the school. Jane's blood froze. Would it strike quickly or wait for when she showed herself? It came again like a haunted thing. Was it lost? Did it need a map to the ocean? Its cry dulled and came in soft, short bursts. She pushed herself to investigate where the playground met the school wall.

Mallory was in the size and shape of the basketball next to him at the foot of the school. He was crying, and tears lost themselves in the blanket of hair pressing his face, in the great roar of the wind.

"Hey," Jane said.

No answer.

"Are you Mallory?"

His voice mixed with mucus, and he croaked, "Wanna go home."

She sat beside him. "It's okay. There's no dinosaur." She didn't know if she believed it but thought it would help.

"Mom."

"We can go inside now."

"I'm cold." His body froze with the same sensation that inhibits deer before car lights, rabbits before predators, and anyone before a plesiosaur, but most commonly rears itself in children when faced with darkness, heights, or the thought of being alone. It stopped Mallory from moving, stopped most words in his throat. His tone was frayed, his body a collection of cut cords.

"Wanna—" he coughed up the rest, inaudible. For reasons unknown to Jane, she remembered in first grade (how much older two years had made them!) when Mallory coughed one too many times in class and puked. He confessed that earlier that day at recess, he cracked open his magic ball and drank the fluid. He puked it all up, and Jane reasoned that was why he was still alive now.

A light shone some ways away to the left, and Jane heard notes of an old lady's voice. Mallory still cried on his shoes, and Jane knew she needed to help him before the lady came, but she didn't know yet how to help with these sorts of things. But she did remember the hugs of her father during the scary bits in the animal shows, so she knelt down now on the balls of her feet and hugged Mallory. It didn't stop any of the tears, but it did cover his head from some rain.

Clomping feet drew near. The dinosaur? The fifth grade English teacher, a woman whose good graces had fled from her looks to her heart, entered the scene. The dinosaur. She had Pierre in tow under a large, black umbrella, and she crouched to Mallory and asked, "Are you alright?"

He didn't answer and bunched his face together, hampering his weeping. Jane took an arm, and Pierre noticed, taking the other, helping or forcing him to his feet. Mallory snuffed his nose, and as he stood, his clothes stuck to him. The first step was a stumble, and every step that followed was stiff, as if Mallory feared falling through the ground, as if he was scared someone would grab him from below and pull him under. He whimpered still as they reached the door, but Jane and Pierre kept him under the teacher's umbrella, and in a moment they could see each other in warm clarity again.

# 5

MALLORY RIFFLED A DECK of tarot cards, an old graduation gift from Chloe, in the cat's cradle of his fingers. Mallory had always wanted them, though he still didn't know how to use them. For as long as he could remember, he busied himself with the future, with hoping for and faux-predicting it, and these cards were his latest foray into the occult. He spent long nights in elementary school alone in his bedroom, sometimes inviting Pierre, sitting over a plastic crystal ball his parents bought him. He would wave his hands over it, shake it, and Pierre would play along, but he always doubted.

"What makes it so special?" Pierre would ask. "What's in it?"

Mallory shrugged. "Ghosts?"

"Ghosts don't talk." He eyed his friend with equal parts horror and concern. "Do they?"

The following week, Mallory crafted a spirit board from printer paper, demarcating its edges with rulers, crayoning the letters in the style of a computer keyboard. He and Pierre traced a pink eraser planchette over it, but nothing came from the endeavor.

"See?" Pierre said. "And why are you talking to ghosts, anyway? How would they know the future? They're dead."

This question frequented Mallory longer than he would've admitted; it came to him now as he shuffled tarot cards in his apartment.

Mallory took great efforts in his formative years to pry something from the ghosts' mouths until he realized it was only a board game, and even after learning the spirits were mute, he viewed the keys and its cursor as an integral part of himself, metonymy for a greater trend toward prognostics: magic balls and spirit boards in his younger years, astrology in middle school (the times he spent with Sylvia, the times he spent alone), and palm reading in high school. Now, he placed the deck of cards on the coffee table.

His open house two years ago, when Chloe gave him the deck:

He hadn't read much about them but held an impromptu reading anyway and, shuffling the cards, dealt one to her. He pulled their other friends from their own conversation to the reading and dealt them in. Looking at the deck on the table now, he didn't remember who pulled which card, and he certainly improvised his auguries around their titles and arts, but he remembered everyone was happy with the carnival trick. Everyone but Jane, who insisted against her involvement. When she was alone later, Mallory asked her what was wrong. The others laughed in the background with groups of other graduates they all housed vague friendships with. Sylvia was not there.

"It just rubs me the wrong way," Jane said. "I don't know."

"Are you, like, okay with it?" She hadn't struck him as religious. "Like...?"

She shook her head. "Magic's fine. I used to watch Penn and Teller with my dad." She looked up at a beam in the pergola, finding words for her argument. "I don't like the future."

"Um."

"I feel like I won't change much. Like, older, but I'll still just be me. There's nothing to predict."

Mallory found this as a light personal attack on his hobby and, finding a hole in the argument, pounced. "Weren't you different when you were little?"

She blinked. "Maybe. But it's mostly bad stuff that's happened. Or I've learned about the bad stuff that happens. If you read my future, and no offense, but you probably couldn't say a lot of good things."

"What if I tell you the bad things?"

She raised an eyebrow. "How much?"

It was another question he couldn't answer, in part because he wasn't trained in tarot readings and couldn't predict to begin with. But he thought about it in bed that night, about what he would do if it all was real and he really could read people's lives, at least small parts of them, like radio channels. If he saw something catastrophic in someone's future, would he tell them, or would he act surprised when it came to pass? He remembered the writing on the wall with Sylvia and wished he told her what would happen, and had he seen their future then?

It was tenth grade, and they had been together for four years. They would stay together for another two. Clearwater High's football team was playing the last game of its season, and Mallory and Sylvia sat in the stands, shivering and swaddled in thin blankets. She hadn't talked much, so he hadn't answered much, and vice versa. It was the last quarter, and Sylvia was fixed on some point in the distance, too high for the field and too low for the stars.

"Whatcha thinking about?" he asked.

She muttered, "Parents."

"What about them?"

She took her chin off her palm. "They still don't want me out past dark. Like I'm still a kid." She yawned. "Said I couldn't come tonight, either."

Her family wasn't new to Mallory, but they always made him uncomfortable. Sylvia and he had similar upbringings, but any resentment Mallory held for or from his own parents left long ago. Still, he rarely saw his parents, and she faced hers daily.

He asked her, "Will you get in trouble?"

"Fuck it. She'll just yell and—" Her eyes widened for a breath but shrunk back to apathy. "Sorry. I didn't mean."

He expected it and said nothing. Someone scored a touchdown. People around them clapped and waved streamers against the wind. "Will you be okay?" he asked at last.

Another pause. A wave was starting, folding through the crowd, sweeping around the couple. "I don't feel like myself."

"What do you mean?"

"Like I'm not me. Everything that *was* me is changing. Like all my friends are gone but you and, and I wish I could stay still." She was shivering.

"What about Chloe?"

"Doesn't talk to me anymore."

His heart tore in equal halves. "Are you cold?"

"No," she snapped, moving his hand away. "Yes. But I don't want to be. All that's ever gonna happen is I'm gonna lose people. I can feel them slipping." She wrapped her blanket tight over her shoulders, over her head like a cowl. "I don't want to wake up, y'know? No more tomorrows, please."

Mallory didn't regret their breakup when it happened, but he did regret losing her in that moment. He recognized he alone couldn't pull her from whatever hole she fell in, couldn't sweep the debris of whatever ailed her, but he tried to think he could. (Sylvia thought he could, and he saw that.) After they broke up, he never saw her again, and Mallory feared the worst but couldn't be sure of anything, and he tried to forget all six years of it, wherein only elementary school remained to look back on and smile. But her memories could never entirely be edited.

A knock at the door. It was seven in the evening now, and Pierre was out getting pizza for the house party; Chloe's debut was tomorrow, and they wanted to celebrate with her tonight. She couldn't squeak out of dress rehearsal, but the plans remained for the others.

Jane let herself in.

"Am I early?" she called.

"I don't think so. Just first." He straightened. "Pierre should be here soon. Don't know about Cecil, but he said he'd come."

She wore jeans and a faded T-shirt emblazoned with a cereal mascot. The apartment was simple: two bedrooms on the far wall with a bathroom between them, a kitchen, and a living room furnished with two couches, the coffee table, and a television. Around the room hung thrifted paintings, and Mallory and Pierre busied themselves at times arguing if these were classical replicas or contemporary work. A small window looked out on the wooded trail leading to the apartment complex.

"I'll text him." She did.

"Hey, do you—" He slowed his words to belie he hadn't been thinking about it. "Do you remember my open house?"

She looked up from her phone, and her eyes lighted on the cards on the table. "You're still into that?" she said, overtly sterilizing any malice in the phrase, like a mother to her son.

"Well, no. I never really was. But what did you say about the future then?"

She frowned. "Probably that it'd suck. I wasn't too bright then."

"You mean 'happy?'"

"Yeah. I mean I'm still not." She hurried to correct herself, coughing a laugh. "But that's fine."

"Aren't you, though?"

She froze, thinking, sitting across from him, the deck between them. "Nothing's changed but the year. Out of school now, but that's not much."

"What about, um." He was at a loss. Was nothing novel in the past two years of her life? "Cecil?"

Jane stiffened again. Cecil's life was a secret kept only with her, but she saw Mallory notice the position the name put her in, and she had to say something. "I mean, Cecil's great. I love him. He's just trouble sometimes."

"What for?"

She closed her eyes a fraction too long as she blinked. "Addiction."

"What?"

"Just"—she searched for something to pin the mistake to—"to people who don't care about him."

"Oh."

She breathed out. "He just gets himself hurt sometimes. It's alright. But he isn't, y'know, a *perfect* life addition."

"But you're okay?"

She was, but she knew she escaped inquiry about him only briefly, so she tilted the conversation. "Mhm. But I'm glad you still like the cards. It's a good gift for the hobby."

He took the bait, and grief drained from his face. "I could try reading you if you'd like."

"How about I flip it and that's that?"

Mallory agreed. Several things happened then: Pierre opened the apartment door, two pizza boxes in hand; something bumped Cecil's car, and a woman fell on the hood; and Jane flipped over the top card of the deck. It faced Mallory, so Jane saw the inverted image of a skeleton looking down the edge of the card at him. Facing Jane was an empty thought bubble. The card was Death, and the moon was rising.

The Vintage nestled between two taller buildings, and its roof was a valley between them.

A fire escape spiraled down three stories, wedged between the Vintage's right wall and its neighboring clothes store. The roof was concrete with vents and pipes growing on its face. Chloe and her fellow players would sit here for lunch break. The sandwich shop across the street was a squat thing which gave an onlooker from the Vintage a window into the street beyond, and the forest beyond that. It seemed to Chloe that wherever she went in town, the forest was always a block away, and when these thoughts forced her psychically closer to the forest and the lake inside, she felt small; not small, rather but too large to hold herself, her body stretching, her mind frantic. No, she wouldn't think of Phoebe often.

She was here one quiet evening a month before her *Hamlet* performance, and the streets were quiet. Rehearsal ended an hour ago, and she and Mallory sat above the town watching the sunset. It was colored a diluted pink, and Chloe couldn't look away.

"Have you talked to your dad yet?" Mallory asked.

The question stung, and she didn't know why. "I'm trying."

He sighed and took a bite of his sandwich. He bought her dinner too, but she hadn't eaten yet. A loose salad spread in an open to-go box, and Chloe couldn't look at it without thinking of her and the same meal she prepared for her every day after school. But Mallory hadn't known her mother's old habits (were they old already?), and the effort made her smile. They shared a lemonade in a large, foam cup.

"He only wants what's best."

"For you." His voice was flat, Chloe thought, disinterested.

"He's important to me. Please give it time."

"I give you time. I just don't want to give him time. He's not a part of us."

She felt herself on the backfoot, her skin fragile and cold. "He's a part of me."

Chloe caught her sun hat as the breeze lifted it from her head. She wore a white dress flapping at the edge of the roof. She wasn't looking at Mallory, and his voice played in her mind as a narrator. They sat together on old beach chairs pressing against the short wall guarding someone from falling to the street. Mallory joked earlier that it was more of a tripping hazard than anything, but he wasn't joking now. Chloe wished he would watch the sunset.

He apologized, said he shouldn't have said that, and asked her how the "part of her" was going, how she was thinking of herself. She never sat in one place and often sickened in her interests, her friends; in her clothes and in her skin; in how she woke and slept and in what she ate; how she breathed, how she talked. She wanted on these ill days to be someone else entirely, to restart. Her blossoming acting career hadn't spawned these

thoughts—they rooted in her long ago, sometime during pu-
berty, she guessed—but reinforced them, reassured her that it
was okay to writhe in herself sometimes. It was art or something, losing herself in what she represented on a stage, losing
herself in something not herself. Maybe this was why she loved
Mallory: she could form closer to him, his interests and his
friends (her card was the Empress, Mallory said, which Chloe
didn't understand, but she appreciated the connotations of an
empress), which gave her a small constant in her lapsing waves.
She held in the midst of her experiences a permanent fraction
of Mallory.

Today, she remembered good things—other dates, school
plays, sleepovers—so nothing rotted inside her. She would remember the bad things, the worst things, on other days, losing
this self for hours in remembering and looping her rememberings. She knew she misremembered as well, that the past
that diagnosed her was reinterpreted differently over time and
iterations, watching this Chloe Barnett say that phrase in a new
light or adding something alien to the sequence altogether,
someone who wasn't there or something that wasn't said, and
why did she care so much for what happened to her, and why
did she let herself care? The sky was beautiful, she thought, but
if she and Mallory ever left each other, this same sky would fill
her as mustard gas.

"Chlo?" he asked again.

"I'm good." She startled. "I'm fine."

"Identity stuff?"

"Oh." She slouched back in her chair and saw Mallory
from her peripherals. He was watching her, measuring her
movements to her emotions like she was a character. The salad
was there too, balanced between the arm rests, watching her.
"Do you think I'm a character?"

He thought. "Do you?"

"Sometimes. I feel like the wrong actor is playing me, though."

"What do you mean?"

"I don't know." She leaned in and drank some lemonade. Mallory smiled, probably, she thought, because this was her first real movement that evening. "I don't know me, I think."

"Um."

"When tomorrow comes, I won't be this again. I don't know. I don't know who I am."

"Well, start at the beginning. What do you remember?"

A laconic suicide note. She remembered the day it happened and the threads spinning from it catching and staining all other memories. But she also remembered those closest to her, those who remained in whoever she was, those who bridged the crevices in her, tugging the rope and bucket to portion memories from a black well. She understood her life to be a war between these poles, the hauntings of one middle school morning and the pervasiveness of a handful of friends. She responded, "Ghosts, I think."

# 6

It was pizza night in the Barnett house, and hours earlier, Jane waited for an invitation in the lunchroom. She had found Chloe in elementary school, had claimed her long before anyone else knew her name. She would call Chloe hers not with jealousy but to remind Chloe that she had someone with her—likely at her arm, as Chloe stood notably taller than Jane in elementary school. Jane was the first person Chloe remembered having a lasting bond with, a bond built at recess with mansions and cities constructed with dirt and sticks. She guarded her from the mean kids (everyone knew the mean kids), swear words, and hallway shoves.

Sylvia was the only other girl Jane allowed in their circle. She shared her favorite subject with Jane—science, where Jane liked the animals, Sylvia the plants—and naturally, they fell in together, fell in with Chloe by extension. Sylvia had first noted Chloe's pizza tradition, which she too now bated her breath for in the lunchroom. She and Jane snuck furtive glances at their friend who shoveled pickles and lettuce into her mouth, glancing between themselves, hoping the other would ask.

It was a Friday in fourth grade when Chloe said, "My mom said you guys can come over today. She's buying pizza."

They nodded in sync.

"I've never been to your house before," Sylvia said.

She sounded, Jane thought, as if she had abandoned their scheme and would refuse the invitation, afraid of entering a foreign state. She smiled to reassure. "It's really pretty."

Chloe kept eating. Then, "Should you ask your parents?" Each word she spoke in elementary school was articulated with the heft and bravado of what she thought actors sounded like. She would recall this quirk with embarrassment, resolve repeatedly to purge this narrative style from her voice, fail to do so, and accept it.

Jane thought her parents would let it slide. She watched a detective movie with her dad last weekend and had been saying "let it slide" all week. But no, she hadn't asked her parents. How could she ask when she was at school?

"My mom says I can, but I can't be out late." This was Sylvia.

Jane looked at her, astonished. How had she asked so quickly? The question was just posed, and in the same moment, she had an answer. Sylvia only blinked.

Jane asked her, "Do you have lights in your eyes?"

Sylvia shook her head.

"Like screens and electricity?" No answer. "Like Jones Bones?"

"Mom says I can't watch that."

"Oh." She dropped it, thinking Sylvia belied some secret spy technology.

"My mom is picking me up," Chloe said. "I can ask her to call your mom."

It was settled then, and the school day's closing hours were ignored. Even science, which had drawn Jane and Sylvia together, was a muddle of attention. Chloe, oblivious to her guests' excitement, paid full mind to story time while they chattered in the back. The book was about a fish giving his colorful scales to his friends, and Chloe liked it because she enjoyed the technicolor prints and the texture on each shard of a fin, sating her mind's appetite with more senses than she knew existed. In science class, she learned that all colors came from the sun, how light bounced around the room into her eyes. That was why, Ms. Lizzie said, you couldn't see colors when it was dark out. Ms. Lizzie pointed to their class fish, a dozen printed guppies, and told the students to watch their colors leave when she turned out the lights.

Someone screamed behind Chloe, and a desperate, sympathetic desire to scream racked her bones in the same way the sight of vomit churned her stomach. But in the same moment, the lights returned, the lesson with it, and that was all of the scream.

On the bleachers in high school, Sylvia confided in Mallory that she was the screamer, though Mallory had no memory of the incident. He asked her why she screamed and if she was afraid of the dark.

"I guess," she said. "I still am. But not like that."

"You don't have to get defensive." He huddled closer.

"Not like a bitch. I just want to see people."

"I get that."

"It's hard to see people if, y'know."

It was the most she would divulge to Mallory in their time together. He cherished it, even if he didn't understand it in full. "When it's dark out?"

She frowned at the pushback. "Out or in."

Nobody looked to see who screamed. When the lights returned, Chloe fixed her eyes on the long windows above their desks. She thought about the sun and what would happen if it never came out again. Ms. Lizzie said last week that Uranus got the least sunlight, three hundred and sixty times less sunlight than Earth, and that it was always cold and dark and nobody lived there, or nobody wanted to.

Chloe thought about the cold solar system until Ms. Lizzie said it was time to go. Jane and Sylvia towed her along to their lockers, to the front entrance, and outside.

The wide doors of the school swung open as its students poured out in the same pattern a wave curls around a barrier. The spring sun scratched their arms, and yawning buses clogged the roundabout. In the crowd of parents waiting on the sidewalk, Phoebe Barnett talked with a security officer.

"Mom," Chloe called, running to her. "Can friends come over for pizza day? I already told them they could."

She left her conversation and rubbed her daughter's head as she tugged on the hem of her gray dress. "I don't see why not," Phoebe chirped. When she talked with kids around, her tone mimicked the warbled staccato of a finch.

"Can—" Chloe glanced behind and saw Jane still at the door and Sylvia in her shadow. "Can Jane call her mom?"

Phoebe's gaze followed hers. "I have her number, it's alright." She pulled Chloe to her waist as she flipped out her phone. As it rang, she whispered, "Jane can come over, I'm sure it's fine. Her mother's a saint."

Chloe ran back to take Jane by the arm, Sylvia following. They stood in a ring around Phoebe.

"...to stay over?" she was saying. When the children came, she glanced at them, bunched her eyes in a smile, and waved at the new girl. "Mhm. Maybe. I'll call you back."

Chloe realized this about her new friend: she hadn't talked much, and while Chloe thought herself shy, she never thought it a fault. But Sylvia shrunk behind her friends when Phoebe smiled at her. She looked at the ground. Something strange was in this shrinking, something Chloe wished she hadn't seen, felt guilt or embarrassment for seeing, like Sylvia had told her every bad grade she ever got, and Chloe could do nothing with the information but wallow.

Two kids ran by with coloring books, bumping Jane, returning Sylvia to her frightened portrait. She looked to Chloe, locked eyes, and despite their budding friendship, Chloe wanted to run. Sylvia turned her legs to stone and lived in Chloe's head—lived, Chloe saw in her swollen eyes, away from Mrs. Barnett, who clicked her phone off and smiled again. "Well who might you be?" she asked.

She didn't look up at her; the question didn't seem to reach her. She possessed Chloe, wouldn't let their eyes part, dug in Chloe's head for answers, for help.

Chloe said, "Sylvia."

"Sylvia Stockton," Jane added.

Mrs. Barnett reached forward to rustle her hair. Sylvia turned her eyes like a hunted thing and, raising her shoulders, accepted. "I'm happy to meet you," Mrs. Barnett said, retreating. "You have a pretty name, Sylvia Stockton."

They left school before the buses. Chloe sat in the front of their car, Jane behind her, Sylvia behind the driver. They passed from the school and around a dozen winding neighborhoods in the town's suburbia. Chloe didn't know it then, but one of these was Mallory's Juniper Heights. Two others were Pierre's and Cecil's streets in similar communities sans third stories. They drove through the heart of town now, storefronts packed close as if cut from one large chunk of stone, and Chloe imagined them cut like piano keys or teeth from the sidewalk. She always thought of them as the earth's teeth, though the metaphor made her squirm. It was an intruder in her thoughts, and whenever she looked at the town's rigid structure, an irresistible urge to check her own teeth ran through her mind, and on touching them, she felt them foreign in her body, uncomfortable.

She did this now.

Phoebe rolled the windows down, and tinny pop music filtered the sighs of the passersby, the laughs, the hollers. Jane picked these out from the sidewalk. Did they go to school, and why weren't they there now? Some were adults, but the bigger kids, didn't they have bigger school, longer school? She looked at the older folks and thought simple things about all the different people in the world and what they, being older, learned in bigger school and how much they remembered from little school. The speed limit lowered, and they passed Jane's house, a tight Victorian thing on a street corner. In a few turns, they drove adjacent to the forest, pulling into a small house across the road from the trees.

The minivan parked in the garage, and Chloe led her friends inside. It was a stuffy house, a house which, in his later years, Henry would think was too small, had too many walls and not enough in them. He was reading in his study when he heard raindrop footsteps inside. He set down his book and dialed delivery.

Phoebe stood in the doorway and waited for the call to end. A cashmere rug caught the edges of the floor, and busy shelves clutched mementos: softball trophies and band ribbons, a book or two, some plants. His desk looked out a window at the side of the room to the front yard and the forest beyond. Phoebe joked every so often that he lived in a stock image. He put his phone down now.

"Good day at work?" Phoebe asked. He worked in "business," which Phoebe imagined as forwarding emails between banks.

"Good enough. I'll be down in a second." He dragged a hand through his hair. Thunder steps ran just down the hall. He sighed. "She's gonna be great, y'know."

She raised an eyebrow. "She *is* great, Henry."

"I mean the acting." He stood. "Are you having anyone over tonight?"

"I think she's as good as she'll ever need to be. And no, you?"

"Well."

"I just know she's our daughter, and that's enough for me." She winked to show lighthearted intentions, but Henry sensed or thought he sensed something nudging behind her words.

He nodded, somehow defeated. "She's our daughter. I'm just excited is all, for where she's going."

Phoebe stepped across the room and hugged him, burying his face in her shoulder.

"I'm not having people over," he said to her arm.

Chloe toured the girls around; rather, she toured Sylvia through the house while Jane peppered comments, thinking or pretending to think she knew more about the house than their guide. She led them upstairs to her bedroom, a cubby tucked above the garage. It was only big enough for a bed, a dresser, and a splattering of posters advertising television shows, musical groups, and detailed portraits of constellations against the florid hues of deep space. Sylvia gazed into these posters as Chloe and Jane started off to the next stop.

"Hey," Jane said.

Her face was empty.

Chloe trilled, "What are you looking at?"

She raised her finger. "What's that?" Her voice was deeper than Chloe expected, and she noted that this was the loudest Sylvia had spoken since they met, the only words above a whisper.

"That's Coral," Chloe said. It was a pink, cartoon fish. "She talks! Have you seen—"

"*That.*" She corrected her, pointing at opaque green and pink curtains above snow-capped bluffs. They curved like bars of music and stood jagged like their notes.

"That's"—she punctuated—"oh-ro-ra bore-ee-alis."

Sylvia's eyes widened. "That's in the sky?"

Chloe shrugged. "Sometimes. Not a lot."

"I haven't seen it before," Sylvia said. "And it's in your bedroom?"

"Can we go to the trampoline?" Jane said. She had asked twice now, but Chloe didn't really want to go outside, so she avoided the question a second time.

"It's just a picture," Chloe said. "You can get a picture of it too."

"I wanna see it. Out there." She turned, still pointing, to the porthole window looking out on the gravel driveway, the forest wall, and the dome of clouds above.

"You can later," Chloe said. She tried her best to mimic Miss Lizzie. "It's daytime now, and you can only see stars at night."

"Oh." She put her arm down and retreated to the poster. "I wanna be like that when I grow up."

"They're still there, though, in the dark. You just can't see them when it's light."

Sylvia again stared expressionless at her new friends. She wasn't fearful anymore, Chloe thought, but acquainted now, comfortable. But Chloe couldn't read a blank face, and how rarely, she thought, did kids at school look like nothing? Only when math was too hard, or when someone didn't know an answer, then they would look like they just woke up. Chloe recognized the confusion in Sylvia as something that didn't add up.

"Can we go outside now?" Jane asked.

If she kept pressing, Chloe would have to give. She asked Sylvia, "Do you want to go outside?"

"Not really." Her fingers traced the northern lights. "When it's dark."

Triumphant again, Chloe turned to Jane. "We can later."

"What'll we do till then?" As she asked, the doorbell rang below. Chloe's shoulders perked as she realized food had come, and she fled downstairs with the others in tow. It was six now, but only Jane noted the time on a clock they passed, and she wondered what they did for the last three hours.

Henry took the white, cardboard boxes from the man at the door, and Phoebe set them on the table.

"Not too fast now," she said. She palmed a salad in a glass bowl, and Chloe remembered this for years: Phoebe Barnett, a thin, short woman cemented against the light blue field of the wall. On her right were the stairs to Chloe's bedroom; to the left, the fridge and so many colored pencil petroglyphs magneted to its rough surface. As time passed after Phoebe's death, this vignette would fade to an impression, its colors blending, its shapes softening until only vague forms remained: a gray rectangle carved with lines of red; a lumpy, brown hill; and a pale mannequin lying in the ocean.

Jane opened the pizza boxes, and she would remember this day eleven years later as she opened parallel boxes at Mallory's apartment the night before Chloe's performance in *Hamlet*. She would look around at Mallory, at Pierre, outside for Cecil who was running late and Chloe who was rehearsing. She would remember Chloe at this pizza night so long ago, would remember she was scared of the dark and how she thought it was weird to be scared of the dark. She would remember that Chloe's mother would die that year and that she, poor girl, would always be afraid of the dark, or would always be afraid of something, anyway, retaining always the character of an ill bird, a quiet thing, a girl lost in an oubliette of history. Jane pitied her and felt her stomach lurch for doing so. She had a right to be wounded. But a vocal part of Jane wished Chloe could forget about it all and start over, and so she was glad for Chloe's career and love life, two starts at someone new.

While Jane pitied her at Mallory's apartment party, Chloe broke against herself at rehearsal. She ran to the roof before her body gave way to vomit, to tears, to her mother, and who was she without her, and who was she with only her, with Phoebe a solitary and habitual tremor in the blood that became her, and she was losing herself, oh God she lost herself, to the diagnostics in her hippocampus, fire in her chest. She was back on in five. She looked at the stars winking like ephemeral dice, and, unable to hold the size of a universe in her thin skull, turned her eyes down to the forest. Glass Lake slept in a break in the trees, and Chloe strained to keep her gaze there. She couldn't fear it any longer; she was the Empress. But after a moment, she broke from that gaze and cleared her eyes. She was on in five and stepped downstairs to change into sackcloth.

AT DINNER IN THE past, Chloe had an idea. Henry and Phoebe were watching something in the living room, and Chloe asked her friends, "Do you want to have a sleepover?"

Something possessed Jane as she convulsed in her chair. "Uh huh!"

Chloe called to the other room. "Can we have a sleepover?"

Henry muttered something, and Phoebe called back, "Sure, sweetie!" A pause. "Should I call moms?"

"No," Sylvia whispered, trapping Chloe again with her stare, desperate. "I can't sleep over."

"Why not?" Jane asked.

"Mom says I have to be home by seven." She looked down at her empty plate, at the crumbs from one slice of pizza.

"But you haven't asked her," Jane prodded.

She shook her head. "I did before."

Still in disbelief, Jane asked, "What did she say?"

"She said I have to be home by seven." She blushed. "And I can do whatever till then."

"Oh," Jane said. She slunk back in her chair.

Chloe turned back to her parents. "Can you call Jane's mom?"

"Sure thing."

"Thanks!" She swiveled back and, fingering the fruit Phoebe scrambled on her plate, decided to eat it later. She grabbed a second slice from the box. Moments passed as they ate in silence, Sylvia watching her plate, and the muffled television played something in the living room. Mom and dad laughed.

"I should go," Sylvia said. She bumped the table as she stood, reciting, "Thank you for having me."

Jane looked at the clock hovering above the front door. "It's only six-twenty."

"I need to go home."

"Oh." Jane stuttered. "I'll see you next week!"

Chloe said the same.

"Thank you. See you." She opened the door and slipped through. It clicked behind her. Chloe and Jane paused their gnawing and looked up at each other, sharing a thought. They hadn't heard a car grumble on the gravel, didn't hear anything drive by at all, and neither of them knew how close she lived. They scraped their chairs from the table and crept to the dining room window like characters in a Jones Bones movie, Jane thought. But when they pulled back the curtain, she was gone. No cars drove on the street, and the sidewalk was empty. A golden glare shrouded the street and surrounding houses as the sun lowered behind a roof.

The moon came within the hour, and it was time to bunker down. They were watching a spy movie as the world turned off. Chloe hadn't noticed the night growing outside, though. She wrapped herself in the film, in Mr. Bones and his lover, in their foreign, quixotic lives, until the credits rolled. Phoebe entered from the shadow of another room and asked, "So where are we sleeping tonight?"

Chloe thought her room would be fun but knew another bed wouldn't fit. The living room? But her parents would be one slim wall away.

"We can sleep outside," Jane posed.

But Chloe turned to the window and didn't see an outside, only reflections of the inside. Here was the living room with its couch, its TV. There was the kitchen, the hall to the stairs, Jane, herself, and her mom. She saw herself most of all in the reflection, saw herself with great clarity in transparent skin against the night. Her arms were too long. She'd never had that thought, but now it scared her that her arms hung too low over the armrest, and her hair was made of string. And she was thin, and she pressed into her arm, her face, felt the bones and hated that she could. She looked like she would die in the hour, and in this space between Jane's suggestion and Phoebe's answer, she expected to.

Chloe felt much younger than everyone at school. She thought herself duller than everyone at school. She felt now like herself in third grade who felt like herself in second grade who felt that her current fourth grade self wasn't adding up, as if by pulling out a single thread of hair, a vertical sliver of her would uproot from the body in a terrarium of veins and arteries. Pulling other hairs would disassemble the vehicle; her body was a garden of thin shards, each tied together at the hair, each with its own role in playing the thin, raw, distressed girl hiding in the couch. She saw this in her reflection against the night, like sticks in a deep lake, and the same slivered woman would haunt her as she grew.

She didn't want to swim in this lake now, but she knew Jane had wanted to all day. Chloe promised herself that they would, for Jane's sake, and they hadn't, which affirmed her in resenting that skeleton girl in the window.

Phoebe said, "Sounds good," and Chloe forced herself to agree. Jane smiled. Phoebe moved back into the shadow, into the storage room held deep within the house. Chloe was scared of that room. "I'll get the sleeping bags," Phoebe called from below.

Chloe and Jane shared the silence. Phoebe resurfaced with the bags, pillows, and blankets, and told them before leaving to her own bed to get her if they needed anything. It was half past eight now, and Jane waited for Chloe to lead her outside. She stood at a sliding door, the precipice to the deck, the dark. Chloe held her breath and took one cold step outside, another to follow, not thinking of the next step, walking through settled dew on blades of grass. They prepared their sleeping bags under the trampoline.

Hours passed there. Chloe spent some time jumping with Jane while they were still energized. She knew it was a distraction, but it worked, and for those hours, she forgot what she looked like and talked with Jane, played house and hotel with Jane, and paved their ways around the yard with flashlights. But Chloe tired before her friend, and now she lay in her bag under stretching nylon, watching Jane's feet jab the mesh like stalactites. The flashlights were off, and Chloe could only see a short bubble around her, everything a dense shadow.

"Did you see Steve today?" Jane said, her voice cracking as she bounced.

"No." A breeze startled the trees, and Chloe shivered.

She kept bobbing. "He's weird."

"Why?"

"He's just weird. But he plays with Pierre. He's nice."

"Pierre?" She posed him as a question, but knowing little about him, Jane didn't answer. More wind came in response. "I'm cold."

"Do you think he's cute?" Jane said.

It was coming back. Her body broke with her breath, her shivering breath in the cold, herself unwinding. She became a puddle sinking into the ground. She remembered the fish who gave all his colors away, who was a lump of coal drifting the ocean, asking her or telling her that colors fade, that they had faded, her colors and her body, that she would crumble one chunk at a time. Something caught in her chest, bit her, heaved in, out.

"I think he's *kinda* cute."

"So cold." She whispered now.

Jane stopped jumping. "What's wrong?"

"Dark," she coughed, fighting tears. The fish left her thoughts and in its place stood Chloe's inchoate profile from the window. "And cold."

A pause. "We can go inside now." Jane unzipped the flap of the trampoline and landed in the grass.

Worming Chloe out of her sleeping bag was a challenge not because she was constricted but from her body wanting and needing to freeze there, to stiffen in her inmost thoughts for reasons she didn't understand and never would, because moving would shatter her, because something told her she would die. She wanted to leave and felt she never needed to. But Jane was at her side, helping her to her feet and flipping on a flashlight, and in a moment, she took her shivering friend to the deck, to the door, and inside.

# 7

CHLOE EASED HER BEDROOM door closed. She thought about talking to Henry again, about finally convincing him about Mallory (and after such an opening, such a performance). But she didn't want to wake him, and was it a show to be proud of? A knot curled in her groin, narrowed her lungs. Phoebe wasn't in the audience. She hadn't come; Chloe's performance failed her.

She would turn twenty-one next month. She was old enough to text Mallory and apologize for the night, say everything would work out soon and don't worry about Henry, say she loved him. But her bones resolved to nothing, and she stood as another ghost, her repeated self with static for blood who could do nothing but think about Mallory and Henry and Phoebe, only and always thinking. In any case, Mallory needed the rest of his night alone, sleeping, gathering himself together again. Chloe realized now that she did him wrong, but nothing more could be done until morning.

Or had she? She said only what she needed to, and now Henry wouldn't roll in his sleep, now Phoebe would be proud. But had she ever been there, Phoebe in the crowd, watching from the shadows spread like moors over the audience, or were her appearances only slips of the mind?

Chloe moved to bed. It was two in the morning, and outside the porthole window, the forest stood as mob in the moonlit, hazy dew. She watched the silhouettes of trees, tried at something beyond, and said goodbye, goodbye until sleep stole words from her lips, and her sun hat fell to the sill.

# 8

Jane woke at six in the evening, and Mallory's house party was at seven. She had been out late the night prior and early that morning watching the stars, talking to Cecil. She asked him again when he woke if he would go to the party, and he again said yes, he would, and Jane was struck with a moment of frail clarity. His dry streak ran two months now, and Jane could tell he cherished the community she and the others grew around him, that he needed to go to the party more than she needed to ask him about it.

They walked through the heart of town as they talked. Every now and then, a car drove past in lonely company, its headlights spreading around the pair as if they had committed some crime and police covered them with hungry flashlights. They walked over the town's bridge while its quick river glinted light from above, and steep banks of moss rose to fences at the sidewalks. The stream fed into Glass Lake, and at the crown of the bridge, only whispers of the river and its intentions could be heard. Jane watched off the bridge into the dark and flickering basin of the stream and its walls and thought she saw a woman move on the bank. But in a blink, it was gone. She rubbed her eyes and yawned.

"I'm just happy things are working out, I guess," Cecil said. "Not 'working out,' but settling down, maybe."

"I wouldn't count it out yet. There's a reason AA gives out so many buttons."

He looked at the sky. "I just feel good is all."

"I'm sorry, I didn't mean—I mean." She told herself to give him this victory. "I'm happy for you too."

He breathed deep. "You like this a lot more when you're older."

She grinned. "We're not that old. And also, what do you mean?"

He shrugged, laughed. "Don't know. Life or something. Nighttime. I just feel good about myself. Like I'm really alive."

"Jesus, you sound like a Hallmark card."


ANOTHER CAR PASSED, AND Jane stood from bed, and let the memory fuzz, abstract. Mallory sent a text hours before to remind everyone of the party, and Pierre and Chloe both responded. Jane typed now, *Sorry, I might be a little late. Lost track of time.* She thought about sending Cecil another reminder but decided against it, decided not to bug him beyond reason, especially for something he resolved to do.

She took her time dressing and preparing for the party, fixing toast and eggs and browsing the internet for a moment. She soaked and tossed her hair, let it fall where it would, and pushed her body through jeans and an old shirt repping what Mallory informed her was a cereal mascot in the guise of a pirate. She slipped on her shoes and left twenty minutes before the party started, arriving before the others in a soft rain and talking to Mallory about playing cards: the past, the future.

Pierre entered then with the boxes, white and grease-stained, and Jane opened them beside a deck of tarot cards and thought of Chloe, how she couldn't make it that night, how her response in the group chat earlier reeked of apology, and she always was sorry that her mother died. But, Jane reminded herself, let her mourn.

Pierre and Mallory busied themselves ruffling through their fridge and cabinets for chips, chocolates, cookies, and arranging them on the coffee table like Wonderland's charcuterie. Mallory stirred a bowl of punch in the kitchen. Jane observed it as she would local wildlife scurrying through a cafeteria.

A knock on the door.

Pierre called for them to come in, and to Jane's relief, Cecil stood in the frame. He wore a polo and slacks, the cleanest outfit she had seen on him, and he smiled as Mallory welcomed him. But his hair was undone, matted where it always curled, and roots of blood grew across his eyes. He sat next to Jane and said hello.

"What's wrong?" she whispered.

He took a slice of cheese pizza and started eating.

"You don't look so hot."

Pierre joked in the kitchen about finding more girlfriends for Mallory so they could throw more parties. Mallory clarified that they weren't dating yet, said she would talk to her dad soon.

"I thought this was nice," Cecil said, looking at his clothes.

"Why does she need to ask, anyway?" Pierre said. "She's old enough."

Mallory sighed. "There's a lot going on. I don't know."

Jane said to Cecil, "It looks good. I mean, have you been crying?"

A long silence. Jane feared he had relapsed, but he always told her when he did. He never wanted to be alone then. As he ate, he scowled at the face-up tarot card on the table and flipped its face back on the deck. "I saw Sylvia today."

"Sylvia." She stared off, remembering. "Oh God."

"I'm alright."

"How's she doing now?"

He shook his head. "A mess."

"That bad?"

He pursed his lips.

"Do you want to talk about it?" But let him think, Jane.

"Am I nobody?"

Empathy stumbled. "What?"

Cecil looked at her now. "Who am I?"

The question was honest, pragmatic. "Cecil Monroe. You're my friend."

He nodded, frowned.

"You'll always have us. You know that."

"Always and only."

"You can make more friends too."

Cecil grabbed another slice, hurriedly broke it into his mouth. "All I am is a friend."

"Isn't that enough?" She put a hand on his shoulder and kept her voice low. The other two still bantered in the kitchen. "What happened with Sylvia today?"

"I don't know." His voice caught. "I don't know."


CECIL SPED OUT OF the alley and onto a main road, leaving her somewhere behind. He didn't look in his mirrors and feared the worst had taken her and she lay hurt or something else in a dark corner. The car mirrors were windows into a grim world, into the bleeding world behind, and Cecil willed his vehicle and all his body inside it to move forward, to move forward. The sun was setting and he wouldn't think of today, and the minutes already dropped behind him, decomposing behind him. But it was the past already. He drove toward the party.

Her fingerprint still stained the driver's side window. He wiped it with a shirt sleeve, felt the print sink into the fabric, and dashed a water bottle on the wound, cleaning. He drove on and took to the radio to distract him from the smudge, the mirrors. It was a pop song. It was a love song. Something in the lyrics made him squirm, and he turned it off. The singer was happy in monochromatic lyrics to be her boyfriend and nothing else.

Streetlights petered out on the long road as it turned to dirt and all became forest. His headlights were lonely eyes in the gathering dark.

He turned on the heat. He was almost there.

Cecil sat alone in his car under the sky. This was familiar: the sky, the feeling that he existed as a planet years from any star. He was accustomed to it, but this was not, for once, the product of addiction. Still, the familiarity of such feelings alarmed him, shrunk him against the car seat, and maybe Sylvia was right about him, or maybe she always had been. He neared the end of the long road, the dark road forming around mechanical eyes, and parked at the foot of the apartments. He breathed in long, slow, and trekked through a light mist to the front door.

# 9

CECIL MADE A NAME for himself in high school, correcting his thoughts to forget the things of middle school and earlier. By sophomore year, he had grown into someone not himself or someone too filled with himself. He had friends now, an advantage absent in middle school, and they brought a vague web of friends-of-friends, a network to remind Cecil that he knew more people than he could consider at any given moment. Everyone who knew Cecil regarded him well or with ambivalence, but never intimately, never recognizably so. He wasn't in any of Clearwater High's sports teams, wasn't remarkably attractive, and he didn't stand out in academia, but the dice rolled in his freshman year landed him in classes with the athletes, the romantics, and the scholars, and by these circumstances, the next year, social renown fell to him. He was even invited to aid the seniors in a prank on Clearwater, teaching them to unlock doors in the school without triggering the alarms. (One reason for his social blooming: he was the first person his classmates met with genuine street smarts.) By senior year, Cecil spent most of his weekends at someone else's house, and as he glanced around each party's retinue, he rarely remembered any names. High school was slipping into the same amnestic patterns of middle school.

Sometimes at these parties, he became a bargaining chip. He would look in nameless eyes and imagine himself casting a chip on the table, on the boat deck, wherever the crowd was largest. He thought he used these people sometimes, used his faux notoriety as a contact for booze, or that they used him as a point of status, saying, "Oh yeah, I know Cecil, great guy, great guy." On a friend's boat one night, he looked in a haze at all the other invitees and their friends, remembering only as many of them as would fit on two hands' worth of fingers, and he could count his drinks that night on three. He grew steadily aware that anybody and not everybody enjoyed him.

A week into senior year, a note flitted through the grate of his locker: *Art club is kicking off at 3:30 today if you wanna come. Thought you might be interested. Don't have to. —Sylvia*

A phone number was attached.

Cecil wasn't a good artist, nor was he particularly practicing, but he took an art class that semester and sat near the girl who signed the note. Sylvia flew in similar circles as he, though she was a much better artist, he thought, and he'd never heard of an art club. For a moment, he thought she might be interested in him (who sends notes in lockers?), but no, wasn't she dating someone?

He texted the number, *Hey this is Cecil. where are we meeting?*

He fidgeted in his locker, started packing his bag as other students walked past. It was five past three now, the last bell of the day ringing minutes before, classes over.

His phone hummed back. *I said the art room?*

It was a tone Cecil only heard from teachers, and rarely then, something outside the world of blank hellos and drinking games. It was caustic, but Cecil smiled, laughed at this unnatural air.

He waited five more minutes by his locker before heading to the room, walking at an escalator's pace down his aisle of the hallway, clapping hands with people in the opposite current to his left, people calling that they should hang out soon and I'll see you later. The lockers he passed were barren and blue. A name tag claimed its spot every now and then, posters well-wishing teams at their events, but that was all. He started to remember something from elementary school but failed to dredge it in full, recalling only his locker and crude handwriting on his nameplate, a declaration: I am Cecil; I am here.

He arrived early to the art room and waited in its hall to enter late as any sane person would do at any social gathering. The art wing was an exhausted place in the dregs of the school, as Cecil theorized all art wings were. White paint chipped off the bricks, and the ceiling lost a few tiles, revealing its wired gore. Replicas of classical paintings and sculptures hung from nails and stood in alcoves in the walls, each surrounded by honored students' work. Cecil thought Sylvia might be on the wall before she graduated.

When he was three minutes late, Cecil pushed past the saloon door of the art room to a funereal sight. The room was dim, and a patina of dust layered the tables, forgetting students had worked there hours earlier, forgetting they would return. White sheets covered drying racks, hunched, dead mounds in rumpled pallor. Four large tables sat in a grid with chairs pushed underneath to hold them in place. Sylvia sat alone in her classroom seat. Her hair was pinned frantically at the sides, and a thin blazer covered the failings of a tank top. A strong jaw cut her chin, and a thin smile followed.

"Hey," she said.

He nodded. "Kinda scary in here after school."

"Turn the lights on."

He did. The dust didn't leave.

"Do you know if anyone else is coming?"

She wasn't very nice, Cecil thought, or at least very polite. The question was flat, more of a demand, really. "No," he said. "I don't."

She frowned now, an honest frown for what he could tell, which wasn't much. The club seemed a genuine endeavor and not a play at his number. "I guess it's just us, then," she said.

"I guess so." He moved to sit at her side, but she stood.

"This was stupid."

Still, he sat. "People will come. Relax."

"If no one comes early, no one will come late."

"I came late."

She readjusted things now, shifted paints and their equipment to their proper storage slumber. "It's fine. I'll see you Monday."

"Why don't we do something small and wait for a bit?" He wasn't sure why he made the offer, but he felt obliged to uphold it.

"No."

"Why not?"

She paused her scattered cleaning. Cecil thought she answered too quickly to think of a reason, but when she did respond, he couldn't dispute it. "It's a waste of time. I only have a few hours before I have to be home."

"Oh," he said. "Sorry."

"Thanks." She finished tidying and turned out the lights as she left.

He sat in the dark. Paintings on the wall turned to patterned dust again, lilting, pastel brushstrokes curdled to veins of mud. It all looked the same dumb slate. Cecil imagined himself stuck in time here, here where nothing moved and light choked in this windowless, subterranean room, and his only companion was his reflection on the table. It was a gross man; it was a man who slouched too forward or backward in his seat, always tired. It was a man who wasn't fond of anything above a good time, and this hadn't irked him until now. Looking at this plain and lurid thing, he witnessed his skeleton and its strata: he wasn't good at anything, and he didn't have enough friends to call him friendly, didn't have anyone he could claim was tied to his life. Maybe Steve would be at his funeral. He was hosting a party in an hour. They would cram onto a pontoon and someone without a boating license would drive to the heart of Glass Lake. It was Steve's parents' boat, and when Cecil asked him what they'd do if something went wrong, he reasoned, "Sell the pieces for profit. Get something bigger." He tapped his temple. "I kinda want to now that you mention it."

Cecil could imagine the boat breaking at the lake's nadir, water growing up the sides, on the deck and up the stairs, and he would float there as the vessel fell below him, fell from sight. And the other merrymakers would float too, drunk and floating, high and alive. Cecil would tread water and see himself in infinite cuts on the surface, see something else, maybe, as he sank. They said you saw strange things if you dove too deep—bodies and trinkets; objects of erstwhile hobbies: pets and paintings and manuscripts and instruments and baker's mitts and sculptures; memories. And would he see today down there, would he see any day, and had he lived at all to prove it? They said you saw all your life in a breath before you died.

"Hey." Sylvia popped back in the doorway. "I have to, like, close the art room when we're done." She tossed the key between her hands.

He blushed, rising. "Sorry. Should've known."

"Yeah."

He grabbed his backpack and met her at the door.

"I mean, you can hang with us, though."

"I'm not going to Steve's today." He had a headache. His body turned against him.

"Steve's?" She started down the hall, and Cecil followed. "Fuck no. I just go for the drinks." She lowered her voice for this.

He decided then that he would follow her to this other "us."

"Jane wanted to catch a movie," Sylvia said. "Horror movie matinée. Chloe's coming too."

"Jane?"

"Clerval. The girl who wears rain boots everywhere?"

Cecil always thought she was odd, though he never talked to her. He shrugged.

"She's cool."

They breached the doors of Clearwater and stretched the parking lot to Sylvia's car, a tight, gray thing accented in the scent of cat urine. She started a quiet drive to the Long Reel. Cecil wondered why she wasn't talking, wondered if she really wanted him to come or if her invitation was only an act of courtesy. They turned through gridded streets and idled through a parking lot. No noises of the town filtered through their windows now. All was quiet, and to break the unsettling frame, Cecil asked, "You're dating Mallory, right?"

"Mhm." She got out of the car, and Cecil did too. The air was dry.

"Is he coming or just the girls?" He didn't know Mallory but tried to hold the conversation.

"Pierre's here." She got out of the car.

He clung to the only name he recognized. "No Mallory?"

"He'll be here." Her shoes crackled against the pavement. "Ah."

She let another thin smile crease her complexion. "And you'll be here, as long as you'd like. If they like you."

He wished desperately that they would like him, but he had no lucid idea who they were. He was drawn to this unfamiliar group for their novel otherness, and when he tried to familiarize them in the smallest sense by asking Sylvia if she thought they would like him, she told him a similarly small "Maybe," and that was all. But he looked at her, tried to read her, and she frowned, morose, and he couldn't tell if this was normal or if she cracked under the weight of his accepting her invitation, and now he would sit as a burden between people who did not want to accompany the popular kid. They would return him to Steve's party, to Glass Lake, and he would watch the waters and ponder how his night would have gone if they had accepted him, Sylvia and her friends, if they had given him a place at the movie.

After the movie, they would go out for ice cream, and Cecil would meet with them every weekend after.

HE SLEPT THROUGH HIS alarm set for prom. It was half past two, and he was to meet the others at three. He didn't know why he slept so late, didn't remember much at all from the night prior, and he chose not to think about it, peeled himself from bed, slipped in and out of the shower, and went to fit on his outfit, a red suit over a plain dress shirt, when his phone sounded against the porcelain bathroom countertop.

*Hey.* From Sylvia. *Can we talk?*

Of course they could. *For sure, but I'm running late*

*Before Prom? Just stuff off my chest.*
*Sure*

The suit was an ordeal to parse through, but Sylvia said it looked good, so he forced it, and he had to admit that he did look unusually good. But he was running late in earnest now, so he ran to the hall, shoved his feet in his dad's dress shoes, and started outside. He lived in the town's heart in one of the tall, thin houses sharing walls with each other, each with piquantly colored faces and small flowers in window sills. At the moment, his parents vacationed in warmer climes, parents who still kissed his forehead before they left. They often spent weekends away somewhere, and Cecil thought whenever they did about what it would be like to be away somewhere, to be in such an alien world and forget Clearwater, forget the lake, forget even his friends if he had to. He thought to forget everything about himself in Europe or South America, change his name, and by then, what would remain? It frightened him, but whenever he found himself on a heavy pontoon, it was a comfort.

He met the others minutes from his home at the bridge. Picnic knolls surrounded benches and tables, diminishing the street in swamps of foot traffic. Other prom-goers met here too, and their outfits imposed glamorously and ironically against their suburban backdrop. Some of them waved to Cecil, and one group invited him to their circle. He waved back and, spying Sylvia at the crown of the bridge, walked on.

She wore a green dress that in another life he may have fallen for. The others stood together in conversation, and as Cecil approached, Pierre welcomed him and started their procession down the bridge. Sylvia and her recruit lagged behind.

"We're going to a haunted house," she told him quietly. She cut her words as if afraid to finish them.

"That sounds alright," Cecil said.

"So lame. Mallory's idea." Her makeup belied a dark heat in her cheeks.

"What's so bad about it?"

Talk floated from those before them: "I never said I *saw* a ghost," Mallory was saying. "Just that if they're real, they probably live here."

"Just..." Sylvia started.

Jane agreed that it *did* sound scary, and Chloe animated with more fervor than Cecil had seen in her, hurriedly clarifying if she could see any ghosts that day, equally mollified as Mallory said, "If you're lucky, I guess."

"Not now," Sylvia said.

"Did you want to talk about it?"

"Stop." She arched her shoulders, balled her perfect hands.

Cecil let it rest. He met other Clearwater students as they walked down the sidewalk, and after trading formalities with passing faces, he noticed Sylvia shifting away from him, closer to the road. She was a third sphere now in their traveling band, Cecil alone and the others in their bubble. One girl stopped to talk with Sylvia, ripping her from orbit entirely. Cecil watched them standing under a lamppost, their attention turning from idle talk to something like whispers, something he couldn't discern as everyone walked on without her. She watched the pack and talked, and shortly, the procession turned a corner.

Cecil filtered into this group now, still on the paranormal and the ethics of ghost hunting. "I've heard some are kinda nice," Pierre said.

"Some people sell 'sex ghosts' online," Jane said. They laughed. "Like, kids' dolls with hot ghosts inside."

"Do you—" Chloe injected, exposed, and her voice was soft. "Do you know how to make ghosts come out, Mallory? Jane?"

Mallory nodded to Jane's handbag from which she pulled a crank-operated radio. "Apparently they can talk through this," Mallory said, "if you flip through the channels fast enough. But seeing them, I guess you just get lucky."

Chloe tugged at Mallory's sleeve. "How would I know if I see one?"

"I mean, I don't really know. If it looks like a ghost, I guess."

"If it sticks around long enough to invite you to dinner, it's probably real." This was Pierre, and everyone laughed but Chloe, who appeared to Cecil as a dwarf planet leaning just beyond gravity. She asked to hold the radio and cradled it in her arms. Cecil wasn't yet comfortable enough to ask her about this, about anything, or to talk to anyone there at all, to be honest. So far were their interests from his, and whenever he quipped into their conversation, his thoughts returned to Sylvia, why she was so stubborn today and where she was now.

The procession stopped where the town ended and the woods began. This part of town was opposite the lake, where houses and streets carved their ways through the trees as arboreal neighborhoods. The elementary school was a short stroll through a road to the left; a walking path to the right led to Clearwater High, where prom would be held. Before them was a path of weathered, uneven stepping stones leading into the forest. Mallory took the helm now, guiding them in single file inside, and Cecil followed in the rear, observing. Before they lost sight of the neighborhood, a creek caught their path. Weeds grappled together in the current, and fluffs of olive moss blanketed the stepping stones across. This river trickled into

Glass Lake, flowed from the town's bridge, and everyone made it to the other side but Chloe. She walked just ahead of Cecil and misplaced a foot on one of the rocks, slipping behind her and following her hands to the water. Her head submerged, but in the same moment, she pushed herself up and onto shore, and those who had crossed already turned now at the sound of her crash to view its result.

She stumbled up the bank and hunched at the river's edge. She searched the water. Blond hair hung straight and covered her eyes, and her black dress clung to her like a Greek sculpture. She was much smaller, Cecil noted, than the dress made her appear.

Jane was closest to her in line. She asked if she was alright, and Chloe nodded. Mallory shuffled back to her and told Pierre to lead now, said that the house was just a little further. Mallory put his suit jacket around Chloe, and they started again on the path. Cecil crossed the creek without trouble, and Mallory smiled back as he did. He was asking her about it all, but her answers were faint.

"Lose your footing?" he said.

Cecil gleaned the word "saw" from the answer.

"Like a fish or a snake?"

"I don't know." She shook her head, and beads of water sprinkled off. "No."

He didn't hear anything more before the house was before them, though it had been reduced to its skeleton of lattice and nails, holes where windows and doors would have stood in the finished product. It looked like construction had just begun, as if nature needed a formal deconstruction to reclaim its property. Rain sowed rot, sponged the floor underfoot. Cecil recognized this place, though he always entered from untrodden paths. He would sit here after school some days with old friends (he referred to them now as old friends with conscious effort) smoking, mostly. They had stapled a hideous old rug to the wood, and scraps of adult magazines hid between the floorboards. An empty mirror frame stood in the corner, the mirror inside having been smashed by Cecil a year or two ago, now scattered across the floor. Chloe stared into these shards. Cecil did too and saw both of their manifold reflections. He pushed himself to ask her what was wrong.

"Nothing." She turned from her gaze to face him. "Just making sure I look good." She adjusted her hair now, fluffed her dress.

He thought she may have been stoned, but she didn't feel the type for it, and he didn't know how to ask, didn't know in any case if he had the right to ask. He knew of a joint hidden in a nook on the second floor.

"Do you think Casper ripped cotton?" Jane said above them.

Cecil looked up to her waving it above the landing, and Pierre climbed the stairs.

"Remember: there's a ghost here, maybe," Mallory said. "Or a few ghosts."

It *was* eerie, now that he mentioned it. Cecil didn't believe in ghosts, didn't believe in much at all, but standing in a decaying palisade of urban life, watching ants filter through the walls, the floor, spoiling months of construction, the entropy unnerved him. He hoped no ghosts watched him now in jealousy of his life, in pity that he should squander it like he had. Cecil's thoughts rattled.

But as Mallory reminded them of the ghosts, Chloe shuffled and stumbled to a side room, somewhere private, somewhere without holes in the walls. Mallory mounted the steps to join the rest upstairs, and Cecil held back to ask Chloe if she would come too.

He stood in the doorway. She sat on her knees, her dress dry but rumpled, facing the far corner of the room. A bright voice curled around her body. Then old music, and more voices and cheering. A cacophony sounded from her shielded lap. She was spinning the dial on Mallory's radio.

Her voice was watery as she asked questions to the air behind her words. "Salad? You said 'salad?'"

He stood in the doorway and struggled to speak.

"Please. Please."

He opened his mouth.

"Say something, oh, say anything."

He turned back and climbed the steps.

They didn't stay at the house for long, leaving for dinner within the hour, landing at a Korean barbeque between them and Clearwater. The room was dim and red, its decorations traditional or offensive, Cecil didn't know. While they ate, Mallory and Pierre chatted about classroom drama or something of that sort, and Jane ventured for the first time since Cecil met her to learn him.

"So," she started, "why are you with *us* today?"

He wasn't ready for the question, and he didn't know if he was ready for his answer. "I think you're cool." He laughed, became amorphous again. "Is that good?"

"Where'd Sylvia go, do you know?"

"No. Off with another friend, I think."

She nodded, chewing. Chloe was staring at her plate, a dinner of mixed greens. "She can be like that sometimes," Jane said as she rolled her eyes. She would grieve this phrase later as she lay awake thinking of how things would have been if she only asked Sylvia the things she asked Cecil, how things would have gone if she mustered at any point an inch of courage and a centimeter of decency to confront Sylvia. How the hour after dinner that night would have changed, how everything in Cecil, like a moth retracting its tornado wingbeat, would have calmed in a steady sea to a happy boy, a boy who had not lost, a boy whose past led to a future with Sylvia, with everyone there.

"You mean Sylvia?"

"Yeah."

He remembered her text. "I just hope she's okay."

"Is she in danger?"

He shrugged, which turned Jane's jocular expression severe. Cecil clarified, "I just mean, like, drinking too much."

She nodded. She knew Sylvia drank too much. Everyone knew. "Do you drink, Cecil?"

He stuttered, which meant he couldn't lie now, at least not completely. "A little."

"How much is that?"

"A bit."

She smiled and returned to her food. "I'm glad you're here, man."

"Same."

"If you see Sylvia tonight"—she thought through a bout of noodles—"tell her, I don't know, tell her something for me. That we can stand by the snack bar and make fun of people if she wants."

"I will. I've been meaning to talk to her anyway." He was embarrassed a moment that he let it slip, but Jane didn't follow up.

"That offer stands for you too. If you're bored tonight, we can stand to the side. Hide a bit."

He nodded, and soon, they were leaving. Plastic boxes were delivered for leftovers, of which Chloe slid most of her meal into. They checked that they had everything before stepping into the warm, spring night. The walk to Clearwater was brief, and all the while, Cecil thought to ask Chloe anything. He wasn't interested in her romantically, but as an enigma, as one who feels entirely inhuman in how she acted, how she interacted with Jane and Mallory and Pierre, as if a disconnect of culture divided them. He didn't know her interests or passions and nothing of her routines, likes, or dislikes, and certainly he knew nothing under the tempered squalls of emotion that her features often reflected. She hid always under a blank and middling face. She was odd, abnormal, but today at the haunted house, she let something get the better of her.

Mallory's and Pierre's attitudes hadn't changed all day, Cecil noted. They were and had been excited about the dance, but had they also gleaned the darker side of that day, the side that barred Chloe in some black world all her own, the side that turned Sylvia from them and dragged Jane to wonder at her disappearance? They must not have, because if they did, they would have confronted or comforted someone somewhere. No, they knew nothing of Sylvia's or Chloe's absence. And Cecil felt similarly transparent to them, as if they didn't note his faults, and he thought to leap on the table and say, "I need you!\" and "Oh, I'm not myself." His heart beat faster, and he feared it. He feared also the faces around him now. They would take him away from himself, would stop all the business in his brain, and who was he without his loud and defining brain? And when they learned to love Cecil, when it all healed, who then would he become?

He hoped now that Mallory and Pierre and everyone else would see him as a lonely man and nothing more. This was what he knew and what he resolved himself to until he became something more, anything in addition. Maybe he could improve his art and become "the guy who paints."

They walked to Clearwater as the far sky flooded red, and the streetlights all at once startled the town alive. Jane talked with Chloe, but Cecil couldn't hear what was said. He busied himself with Mallory and Pierre, talked about school drama he knew far too much about, dirt even from the graduated seniors of years past. He didn't really want to go to prom anymore, a feeling exacerbated as they neared the school and he distracted himself from the others and refused to acknowledge that Sylvia would be there, and why was he worried? But now they stood in the parking lot, already across it, handing tickets to the man outside, stepping into the foyer. The room was dark and smelled of wrestling chalk loosed from the body. The doors to the gym on the left stood open, and pop remixes blared loud enough inside to slur the lyrics. Lights from the gym flashed faster than the eye could process, lighting everything in technicolor stop-motion. A few socialites stood just inside drinking something, silhouetted in rainbow flares. Everyone joined the storm but Cecil, who was pulled back from the group and into a corner of the foyer. He stood as two shadows in the neon dark with Sylvia.

"Why haven't you texted me?" she asked. She sounded sad, Cecil thought, or drunk.

"I thought you were with..." He dug for the name. "Rachel?"

"I am."

A pause. "What's up?"

Beams of light tore her face. She was looking down. "You guys don't talk to me anymore."

"Didn't they invite you to come hang today?"

"I just go and I sit there and there's nothing." Her hands waved around her. "They don't say anything to me. Mallory either."

This was new ground, and Cecil didn't know how to respond. "Do you want me to talk to him?"

"It's too late." Her throat welled. "God, it's too late."

"Have you brought it up before?"

She leaned forward off the wall. "So you're siding with him?"

"What? No, I—"

"It's been months. He hasn't said anything—important?—in months. And now that we're *here*, I guess, none of you have."

"Just let me talk to Mallory, it'll be okay."

"You don't get it, do you?" More frames of pink and blue. Syvia stood like a predator, leaning, her body hanging on itself like the nightmare shadow of a mouse on the wall. Other high schoolers nervously glanced their way as they walked into the gymnasium. "It was never about you. It's about you and her and him and all year!"

"What?" He took a breath. "We're not trying to ignore you. We can always talk more, hang out more."

"Oh, and do what? Play truth-or-fucking-dare like a fifth grader cause Jane won't grow up? Go to a—a *haunted house* cause Chloe can't handle her shit?"

The prey was wounded. "We were having fun."

"It's not our fault, not my fault her mom's dead."

"Too far, dude."

"That's all you have to say?" She heard her voice too loud and recoiled. She spoke now in somber nostalgia. "That's it, then? 'Shut up and move on?'"

"I never said that."

"Yeah." She sighed to herself. "I know. I thought you were different, though. Just fuck off."

He moved to grab her arm, to say something, to do anything to keep her here in the stuffy, variegated air, to make her know that they could change or that they changed already. But as he moved, she clutched his arm, clawed it, leaned into his ear. She said without a whisper, without a howl, a modern curse: "You will never forget me."

She left the school. Cecil watched her go. The song ended then, the lights with it, and in the instant, he could see nothing but her shrinking shoulder blades in the moonlight. He would get used to this moon and its primal gray. Afterward, he would forget on occasion that the sun was out, that he was himself, Cecil Monroe.

At prom now, he watched her until he couldn't. Then, he thought to find a drink somewhere. The party resumed. Cecil entered.

# 10

THREE MONTHS STOOD BETWEEN Chloe's first *Hamlet* rehearsal and its debut. It was summer, and while time passed quickly for the occupied Chloe, the season was a doldrum for Mallory, who recently confessed his affection for her, who recently found these affections reciprocated. He spent several hours every Friday with her, because this was what Henry allowed her: one night a week outside of rehearsal to spend as she pleased. In his vacant days at his and Pierre's apartment, Mallory scraped by being alone. He worked a few hours every day at a sandwich shop across the street from the Vintage, which only pulled his attention closer to Chloe and farther from himself, imagining through his ennui what she was saying, how she was rehearsing. Friends found jobs too, if only small ones, which stressed availability for gatherings and collective outings. Life sped up after high school only to slow down on the daily, what-is-today-for scale. Mallory started digging into the occult again, pulling the fortune tellers he had stashed in his dresser, elementary things like "psychic board games" and more traditional arts. This is where he rediscovered the tarot cards Jane gifted him as they ended school two years ago. The pack was open, but the cards lay pristine inside, stuffed in his dresser under layers of old clothes.

He still hadn't learned how to use them, but when he went online for instruction, something suspended his fingers on the computer's keys. He was scared, maybe, but he didn't understand what caused this fear. In any case, heat lit his chest whenever he thought to learn. Dread would seep through his cracks, and still ignorant to its source, he would think the whole thing stupid, and he would never study and comprehend it all anyway. Starting begot confusion; confusion, disappointment; and disappointment, rejection. These thoughts barred him. It was better to be hopeful in his current lack than to experience this thing and regret the effort.

But relationships were a continued balm in empty days. Mallory got off work before Pierre, and every day became a wait for his friend to arrive at the apartment (two to three hours after him). They didn't spend much time together on any given night, but having another warm body in the home helped him forget the fear and isolation of beginning.

Pierre worked lighting at the Vintage and would often relay blithe marks between Chloe and Mallory. She joked today that the pulleys and the players on stage both had a few springs loose, and Mallory didn't know what to send in reply. He hadn't replied through Pierre for a while. Mallory texted or called Chloe on any conversations they had outside her free day, and he couldn't think of anything simple and airy to continue their game. He wanted to say something plain or cute to bear wind under her feet at rehearsal, but the same vice that clamped him from his hobbies overcame him when thinking of something clever for Chloe, and ultimately, he submitted to the rack.

The others: Jane led a quiet barista job at the Morning Grind. She initiated most of their get-togethers in the group chat, and wherever anyone planned to meet, she would appear.

As such, Mallory spent a lot of time with her, including her early arrival to the house party the night before *Hamlet*. Everyone would watch cheap movies in their apartment, play old games, or walk through the woods circling the town, circling Glass Lake, but these nights came infrequently. Cecil worked at a thrift store now, a low, stuffy place with racks of clothes crammed close enough to warrant a fire hazard. As Mallory walked with him and Jane once through the woods, he asked Cecil how the job was going. It was just past midnight. Cecil said it was all good, but he never afterward talked about his job or what he did outside it. His discussions were always of others, which Mallory didn't mind, though Cecil as an individual grayed with each meeting.

Presently, Mallory stared at the wall and waited for Pierre to come home for the night. The clock ticked to six—one more hour. His eyes drifted back to the tarot cards on the coffee table. He slumped on the living room's couch, eying them, eying the door, flickering. He grabbed the cards now, opening the box and creasing the lid, fanning through them. Their illustrations were gothic: dark reds and sharp angles, life in taut, macabre strings. He could guess at some of their meanings, but others held muddied titles like the Chariot or the Tower. But he knew what they were for—and to think he was somewhere in these cards, in his palms! To think everyone who ever lived and died was a Moon or a Fool, and he slipped their glossy skin through his hands as an ignorant god. This excitement drove him to the occult and the fantastic so many years ago: not the sensation of godliness, but of his inclusion in something beyond himself, a vast web in a greater network. He connected each card in this net, and in this connection drew nearer to the inmost pulses of those around him, friends and otherwise, which always turned his attention to that romantic bond in its infancy.

He texted her now. *Do you want to do something tonight?*

She answered later that hour. *Would you like to? It's not Friday.*

*Yeah, if that's okay with you.* He thought of something simple now. *If you're doing alright too.*

They agreed to meet at the lake.

They hadn't visited Glass Lake together since the *Hamlet* business started, and never had they gone alone together. Mallory had asked plenty about the lake as a date locale, but she always rejected it, brushed it aside. They had been alone enough, so he assumed it wasn't for awkward fear or discomfort. But still she found alternatives, and Mallory asked again now about the lake, almost as a joke, surprised when she agreed.

He stood from the couch and found his body richer than before. He still held the tarot cards, and as he set them back, one fell from the pile to lie face-down on the carpet. A hand parsed forward for the lost piece but stopped at its edge. This one was special, Mallory knew beyond belief and he stood suspended, distinguished. The card was him, not in its exit from the pack, but in whatever details and connotations sketched themselves on its downturned face. But he could go no farther than the back's brocade edges.

Maybe something Jane said kept him from looking. She wasn't fond of any of this, Mallory thought, scanning the room for his other tools, and she might think less of him if he put all his personal weight into a playing card. Or perhaps Chloe stopped him, and anyway, he needed to leave. A hole in Mallory, a great trench spanning his figure, arteries, capillaries, blared commands for his fingers to curl, to pick and pry and witness the real Mallory, the veritable Mallory, the remains of a village cobbled into one boy. Answers were here; respite was here. But Chloe would be waiting. He set the card back on the deck and stole away from the apartment with his backpack.

The air was cold and quiet, and the sun fell as a red band fading by the minute to purple, to black. An iron gate sagging with rust tried and failed to halt vehicles from the forest trail sprouting from the apartments, and Mallory climbed over this to the beaten path. The lake was only a ten minute's walk, he guessed, but Chloe would be there before him. He flicked on a flashlight and started in.

Glass Lake: a patch of ink within painted wilderness. Trees and draped vines clung to their color as they drifted to night, to sleep, to black, and waterborne flowers and weeds clogged the shallows growing wider with the erosion of passing seasons. Mallory stood at the shore and saw himself in the water, a man of shards against the reflected moon and stars and fireflies. He regretted leaving that tarot card unread, antagonized by the imprecision of his name and face in a world of lines and definition. Then another face joined him in the reflection and frightened him out of it.

"Oh, sorry." Chloe wore a jacket and leggings, hair dragged in a bun. Mallory assumed her backpack contained some sort of costume.

"Hey, hi." He recovered. "Rehearsal went well?"

She shrugged and smiled. They talked on shore about the production, about the other players and Pierre's backstage authority. They talked about the play, a script Mallory hadn't read, a story Chloe toyed with in their conversations, explaining wildly false things about its characters and scenarios, laughing to prove which of what she said were jokes and which were genuine. Mallory told her what he had been doing recently, mostly what he hadn't been doing, and convinced her he got outside more than he really did.

Chloe motioned to the boat buried in the dirt, wrapped in vines, and asked if they could try. It was a wooden skiff fit for two, and with the sail gone—likely scavenged, post and all—a pair of oars hidden in the shell would push it along. Mallory was again surprised at her eagerness around the lake, and he agreed. They worked to break the boat from nature, exhume it from the hard earth, surfacing it when they found leverage, examining the body: a few stains, but from a cursory glance, nothing damaged. In the following silence as they observed the juvenile wreck, Mallory remembered the days they all crammed inside after school and imagined themselves far from the lake and the town and into some recurring pirate fantasy.

Chloe asked if they should launch from shore now, and carefully, they brought the vessel to float midway down the dock. Past that point, rot had eaten most of the pier, unstable now and printed by the memory of Chloe years ago, Chloe at the edge of the dock, Chloe and the moon. The two slipped off their shoes and socks and rolled up their pants to climb aboard. A wobble, but no apparent leaks. Mallory grabbed the oars and, facing the shore, cast at intervals heavy strokes against the water. Ripples battered the hull, calming in the same moment, and Chloe stared into these disruptions on the surface, into the lake when it stilled and when it splashed and rippled again. Mallory joked with her about the folktales he and others told about this place so many years ago, and Chloe laughed now and again, glanced up, added whatever details she could, and smoothed her gaze down again to the port now, to the starboard.

Glass Lake plumbed thirty feet at its deepest, and they floated somewhere around there. Bugs screamed on its shores.

"I have something for you." Chloe reached for her backpack. "Maybe you've forgotten it." She unzipped her bag and pulled out a small crank radio.

Mallory's eyes lit. "That's where it went? How long have you had it?"

She shrugged. "Two years. Since prom night."

"That long?"

"Take it." She pushed it forward. "Please."

He did. "Where did you find it?"

Chloe stared in sharp silence, and Mallory regretted his asking and regretted even his curiosity. He had never seen her so still, so resolute in whatever thought housed behind her eyes, that he lost his words, relieved when she interrupted the lull herself. "I just want to check in sometimes."

"Check in?"

She wouldn't say it.

"Oh." He knew it would resurface sometime but put off confronting it himself, delayed asking Chloe about her, and now she forced the issue. "Look, I know it's hard," he said, "but you have to let go sometime."

She pulled her knees to her chest.

"Did she say anything?" He would remember this as the wrong thing to ask, and recalling this moment would hold him awake at night just as Jane with her memories.

"I—" a cold wind disturbed the water, and she bundled tighter. The phrase continued as distinct, frozen words. "Do not have to."

Mallory placed the radio beside him. "Um."

"Change a lot." Her shifting eyes found solace in the sky. "But there's always something that stays, right?" Her arms wrapped around her. "Something that will always be in some-one so that I can say, 'Mal? He's that witchy kid.' You'll always be, oh I don't know, supernatural. Why are you the witchy kid, Mallory?"

He didn't have an answer, and he couldn't find one in time.

"Is it about death? You don't know what's out there?"

His mouth opened and closed without sound. "Nobody does, maybe."

"Or does it give you friends to talk to? Did you have ghost friends when you were little?"

"I guess." Her tone was sweet, understanding, but Mallory could only be offended. He did spend the nights of his formative years alone in his room watching VHS tapes of old magicians and Caligari's pointed shadows, and at the heart of it all, the motif of all his shards, he was alone. He didn't talk to anyone dead just as he rarely talked with anyone living save Pierre and Jane, and as the years crawled by and more friends came, this theme never diminished in him, and with its continued haunting, he continued his investment in ghosts, fortunetelling, and something beyond himself.

"We all have something we can't escape."

Mallory shivered, naked under thin layers of fabric and flesh. "And?"

She said it now with reluctance. "Phoebe."

He nodded. "But it's still something to fight against, yeah? Even if it never changes, it's worth trying to move on. The trying feels better."

She smiled and frowned and smiled again. "I know. I'm giving it back. Saying goodbye, I think. But—please let me check one final time?"

She reached for the radio, and that hunger, familiar desperation, filled her eyes and strung the cords of her shaking limbs. She returned to old habits, habits she had only now denounced, and stabilizing her in this would entrench her further in her cycle, in her stubbornness, in the maternal specter living in her margins. Phoebe had dominated large spans of her life, and in these times, she couldn't enjoy acting, couldn't relish her friends, couldn't live in the woman she became or realized herself to be. She stagnated, and these symptoms worsened now on the boat.

He said, "I don't, I mean, it's not safe."

She glared again, and his lungs filled with acid.

"I just mean that, like." Empty words stalled her progress. "If you want to be happy, you need to stop. Even if it *does* come back."

"One last time let me try."

"You can't relive it."

"She's my mom."

"She *was* your mom."

They were still, and the world around chirped and croaked and screamed and lived and died in the silent screams of night bugs.

"She's gone, Chlo."

She started crying. Mallory caught himself between relieving Chloe's hunger and relinquishing the radio or doing what he could to embrace her now without it. He did both, taking the radio with him as he moved down the boat to hug her. She cried louder as Mallory cranked the radio beside her and nothing came but static and words lost from their contexts. She wept a clashing wail to oppose the tide around them as Mallory hugged her. He set the radio beside them and let its handle spin down and down, white noise falling again to Chloe and the world.

"She's gone," he repeated, and they rested.

Mallory sympathized but could not cry. He felt his own inevitabilities encroaching again, worsened with the paranormal absence on the other side of the radio. Rarely had he heard anything from that radio, and when he did, hours of waiting preceded it. He was beginning to believe there were no ghosts.

Chloe quieted soon. They talked on the boat again, and Mallory perceived a weight extracted. He stuffed the radio in his backpack, a hot skull grappling his mind for attention, a hot skull, he imagined, burning through the nylon. And above that skull rested a gift—a sun hat—which Mallory exhumed. It was a wide, white thing constructed with paper straw and a thin black bow tied around its base. He handed it to Chloe who tried it on, told Mallory she loved it and him and would wear it ritually from then on.


SHE REMEMBERED PHOEBE WITH recurring finality, knew that she didn't know her anymore. But as she looked at Mallory or acknowledged the crown she wore, she dislodged herself from the past, herself, and something eternal. When she relinquished herself, the sun grew again, and she knew she was alive in the present world with its present wonders, no longer a pocket unto herself.

It was getting late. Mallory rowed back to shore.


CHLOE OPENED THE DOOR to her house, her childhood home, a place she wanted at some point to move out of, just past midnight. She walked to her room above the garage, slouching her duffel bag against the wall and heading to the kitchen to cook something small for the night. The dining room stood in her path, its lights on, and Henry read inside.

He put the book down when she entered. "Out late tonight," he observed in a barbed subtext only his daughter understood.

"Yes, and you?" He was always asleep by now.

"Waiting for you."

She moved to the kitchen, and he caught her at the door. "Where'd you get that?"

She'd forgotten to take off the hat, forgot it was an accessory and not inherent to her body. "Mallory gave it to me."

"Mallory?" He chuckled and repeated the name in spiraling severity. Chloe moved to the kitchen and began frying an egg. "You still see him?"

"I do," she called from the other room.

Nothing more came until the base of the egg formed in the pan. "Don't you do that on Friday?"

"Usually." Chloe feared Henry would uncover more of her affair; the soul behind his voice shook whenever Mallory was mentioned. As such, he started every sentence slow, inquisitive, ready to dart to some safe hole in his thoughts if things went poorly.

"One night a week. Remember?"

"I do."

"But, oh, I don't know," he started. "I don't know. I don't know."

She put bread in the toaster. "Are you okay in there?"

"Well. I just don't think he's good for you right now."

She knew his opinion—he repeated it every week—but listening was another twist of the dagger. She loved Mallory, or she thought she did, and whenever Henry reiterated her responsibilities to her craft, she caved more to his side of things, to remain as friends until her feet were planted firmly in the theater business, a prospect fast approaching.

"There's a lot going on right now, and you're still getting used to it all."

She couldn't argue against it. Instead, she said, "It's only a month or so of difference. Either we make things official tomorrow or next month. *Hamlet* is at the end of the month, you know."

The toast popped, and the egg popped inside itself. "You still have responsibilities."

"I'm in the play," she said, plating her food. "Our first show is in a month, and our last is a month after that. Then I can pick roles in other Vintage productions, roles in other theaters, and go from there." She walked to the dining room, wanting to walk past it but knew she had to stall until the conversation ended. He was fragile and would break if she left early in a huff. "This is all I can do. What more responsibility do I owe?"

Henry thought at a blank spot on the wall just above her head.

She was responsible to herself in her career, and she was responsible to Mallory should they turn serious. These were the obligations Henry spoke of openly, the obligations spilled with such surplus on their daily conversations that Chloe was sure she could recite his lecture if called to. But Chloe knew of other commitments in abyssal tides, things she knew Henry grabbed at now, finding palatable phrases for them. These were the obligations to him and Phoebe: first the requirement to make Phoebe proud, then the need to keep Henry company, to keep him loved and happy and so far from an empty home.

Chloe didn't know if Henry knew about this latter bit of himself—that he kept her here of his own interest—but regardless, these were the unspoken responsibilities passed from father to daughter.

He landed on something vague enough to encompass it all and not draw attention to the ghost in the room in her chair at the far end of the table. "For the family," he said. "Responsibility for the family."

"She's gone." As it left her mouth, she wished to rescind it. A wave of hot confusion and embarrassment swept through her as Henry began to cry, and she herself was still getting used to it, would maybe never be used to it. She wanted to break down with him, but one of them needed to keep composure for the other, a precedent. "She's gone." Her voice warbled. "I am doing my best."

"I know. I know."

He sat for a time with his head in his hands, his head in his crumpled fingers, his head in Chloe's old, tired cradle. Above the empty chair at the end of the dining room was a pair of windows, the same windows she and Jane watched for Sylvia through so many years ago, and the hum of streetlights lit the yard, the sidewalk, and the stifling presence of the forest across the way. She didn't feel like Chloe Barnett then, and still she wished to be someone else in other skin and other thoughts in some other place.

"Please just wait a little longer, Chloe," Henry said. "Please, baby. For me."

She retreated to her room to eat and think.

# 11

THEY WENT SKINNY DIPPING after graduation. Two hours had passed since the ceremony, and Mallory and Pierre held a hushed conversation just offshore with Cecil who sat under the trees, dry and clothed. Jane had driven him here from a lurid party with the other high school notables, and the boys in the lake were already whispering when Cecil and Jane arrived. Just inside their sight sat Chloe at the end of the dock tapping a toe in the water and reading the waves with a towel around her waist. Jane sat next to her, filling the last plank, and looking out at the lake from the tip of the dock made Jane imagine she was floating, suspended. The air breathed clear, and the moon tinted everything in dull luster, luster that, Jane thought, made everything appear as if in a dream. And in the lake was another moon, more brilliant and terrible for its closeness. This image wavered as Chloe tapped her toe.

Jane said, "Too cold?"

A fish swam under the disturbance, swam away.

"I mean the water."

"Oh" was all Chloe said, and Jane thought she only now recognized her presence.

Chloe's hair was different. In place of her once-sweeping blond fashion was a short, jagged cut. It wasn't a bad look but a startling one. "You got a haircut," Jane commented.

"I gave one." She was flat.

"To yourself?"

She nodded. Infant ripples traced the water's surface. Chloe laid her head on Jane's shoulder in a moment of emotion the latter had rarely observed in her. She was always reserved, and even in this quiet act, she held something back. But it was a start at weakness. Her cheek was cold.

"It's cute," Jane said. Chloe's weight pinned her right arm to her side, so with her free hand, Jane ruffled her hair. "Doing alright, hun?"

She breathed long and swallowed hard, and Jane felt it wrack through Chloe's body and into her own. "Not fond of swimming."

Jane tried to sound bright but knew the effect was tactless to whatever mood hid in the scene. "You can chill with us by the shore. I can get your clothes for you."

Slowly, Chloe shook her head. She held Jane there for a bit, and even though Jane didn't add anymore, she prided herself as Chloe's chief confidant now, someone of emotional reliance in whom Cecil alone confided in her to that point.

"Do you know how many people drown every year?"

"What?" Jane stared at the sliver of face she could see against her shoulder, but nothing seemed out of its calm normal: no crying, no jagged breaths, only tired eyes piercing the water. "I don't, sorry."

"And how many suicides?"

Panic sprouted. "What's wrong?"

She pulled her feet from the water and shook them dry, shook them away from her body and cringed at the droplets. Her knees pressed against her chest. "Just thinking."

"Do you need someone to talk to?" Jane tried to keep her own emotions stable, but the apparent urgency filtered her words through a layer of fear. "We can—"

"It's alright," she reassured. "I'm alright." Her words caught in her legs, and she turned back to melancholy, to resignation. "They never found her."

It struck Jane, Chloe's new confidant, as the key to the past. Every day with the group where Chloe diverged as a listless, wordless pole, and every non-answer to probing questions, and every day she was busy: everything about this scrawny, abject actress was with doleful regard to her mother, a woman whose death Jane thought had stopped affecting her sometime in early high school but saw now that it founded deeper roots.

And the panic faded; Chloe was only remembering. Jane held her tighter. "Thinking about it tonight?"

"*Her*," she corrected.

Water splashed in the shadows behind them. Mallory and Pierre left the water.

"We haven't talked in a while," Chloe continued.

"Yeah." Jane smiled and nodded, her head rubbing against Chloe's matted hair. "We should change that."

"Not us."

"Her?"

Chloe nodded.

"I think she'd be proud of you." Jane turned briefly to see the others redressing.

"It's not about that." She shook her head. "I don't care if she's proud. I don't care how she feels about my grades. Or what I do now. And I don't care if she's one of those stars looking down thinking, 'That's my girl' or 'I'm proud of you.'

I know I'll forget her again and I'll keep forgetting her, and whenever I do, I don't remember how proud she would be."

Jane didn't know what to say to a flood. Chloe answered for her.

"All you can do when you're dead is wait around in memories, coming and going. All your pride and love and—" She caught her breath. "It all goes with you. I feel sick."

All this was beyond Jane, who at first steeled herself in comforting her friend but now knew that years of the dead piled against the door, threatened to break Chloe in some kind of episode, so she resolved to tide things over until she could approach her in less neurotic terms. Here on the dock, she could only hope to mollify the grief stuffed so tightly and sincerely into her bursting frame, to withdraw Chloe's eyes for a moment from whatever she saw in the lake, from whatever memorial frames reflected in the water. Jane looked around and was relieved to see the boys huddled by a tree, talking and waiting.

Jane made a note to talk to her again soon. She said now as an escape for her and Chloe both, "While we drove over, Cecil mentioned getting shakes together." He hadn't, and she would need to improvise this with the others when they returned. "Would that be nice?"

Chloe sighed. "Yes and no." She stood and wrapped the towel around her.

Days later, months later, years later, Jane would wish she had hugged Chloe. She would wish a lot of things changed in that moment and in dozens of other places in time, and she would roll in bed and check the clock and imagine herself doing these novelties and fixing everything that grappled her in and to her bed. But it would all dissolve, going and going, into loud, silent mistakes.

Jane walked to shore before Chloe, changing back into her clothes in the shadows, and as Chloe did the same, Jane explained to the others that they were all going to go for milkshakes to end the night.

# 12

THE THEATER TEACHER AT Highland Winters Middle School stood in a cone of hard light. Her name was Mrs. Lavine, and she addressed an audience: "Good evening, everyone, and thank you all for coming. As you can probably tell, we've been working quite hard for a few months." A hand motioned to props waiting for stage lights to expose them, oversized mushrooms and technicolor streamers forming a rainbow canopy. "None of this could've happened without all you parents out there and..."

Pierre and Chloe sat backstage with the rest of the crew. Their clothes were entirely black—a look Chloe resented—while the cast in their costumes occupied a separate social bubble. Pierre played rock-paper-scissors with someone else on the team, and Chloe was stuck inside again.

She would coin the phrase "stuck inside" years later during a Friday night with Mallory. It was something, she would say, she did a lot when she was younger, something she occasionally slipped into still. She would think for too long with such little attention to outside stimulus that reintroducing herself into the physical world became overwhelming, and her voice would drown in its conscience. In this mute body, she watched everything behind two stolid windows. At the play now, she saw Pierre play rock against paper; a tight, grainy television screen broadcasting the current happenings onstage; and Alice and the white rabbit tucked behind their respective stage wings, ready for the lights. Alice, a role played by a girl Chloe didn't know—and now that she thought of it, she didn't know many of the people she performed with, didn't know many people at all—stood just a few feet from Chloe, and bitterness swelled in the mute girl. She leaned forward just to be nearer to that outfit, that character. But as Chloe's thoughts changed, so too did her posture revert.

She hated Mrs. Lavine. She wouldn't have said it in the moment, and looking back, she never found the reason for her disdain, but all the same, she loathed her. This unbroken enmity formed a new set of emotions for the fresh teen, emotions which wouldn't recycle themselves on anyone else in Chloe's life save chance outbursts against her father in the years following high school, outbursts she would pleadingly apologize for moments after. In those afteryears, Chloe realized envy might have driven her hatred for Mrs. Lavine. She had given someone else the part of Alice and doled out only a stagehand to the hopeful Chloe. But she was still in the show, and she tried to stay hopeful.

Pierre won now and lost again. The screen above still displayed Mrs. Lavine's rambling figure, and Chloe tried not to think about her.

"Without further ado, I formally welcome you to Wonderland."

Applause. The spotlight was stuffed, and the teacher strode past Chloe and the others, waving, whispering to the actors.

The stagehands' outfit was perhaps another reason for Chloe's disgust. She went out with Henry the night before when she realized she didn't own anything to fit the dress code:

black clothes, clothes to hide in. She unearthed baggy leggings and a sweatshirt from the general store at the end of town, both dark gray, but it would have to do. And her hair was forced in a bun, those blond curtains she loved to sit behind. Chloe felt as she had at the sleepover four years ago (and had it been four years?), how she felt several times between then and now.

She was small. She was too small, and these clothes hung heavy around her, made her light by comparison. She wondered again what would happen if she tugged too hard on any loose string—would the body give way, and what would she see in the fresh hole? Looking in from where an arm once was, could she see the heart? And from an ear removed, could she spy the brain that caged these thoughts, the brain that proposed now to disassemble her and replace the parts with better ones, cleaner ones, parts that weren't so thin and small and familiar? To be anyone else was the end she worked toward. A different girl, maybe a better girl, wouldn't lose herself inside. A different girl would be made from wholesome stock, come with stainless memories, and would be better, be well.

Chloe thought she spent too much time remembering, and she returned to this verdict during middle school and most of high school, dwelt on it, quarreled with its validity, scraped the walls of her faculties, her vessel, never committing to an answer.

But she was stuck in this stagehand, and the show was starting. The screen above displayed a blond girl sitting against a tree, her outfit a white and blue blouse that Chloe knew was resized for her. A boy in a rabbit costume pulled a watch from some fold in his fur, saying, "Oh dear oh dear, I must be late."

"What, wait." Chloe muttered the lines to herself before Alice echoed to the crowd. "Oh dear."

Pierre tapped her shoulder. "You know this part?"

She hadn't noticed his games had finished, and he too watched the screen. She nodded and turned back, whispering, "Now where has that rabbit gone?"

He tapped her again, pulling her outside, crossing the precipice. "Are you alright?"

"Yes."

"You sound tired."

Chloe wanted to say something, but as quickly as she returned to the world, she receded behind her eyes.

The play continued into Wonderland, and Chloe and the crew wheeled various props onstage while the lights shut off. Chloe was in charge of one mushroom, a tea table, and a painted backdrop. While they waited like firemen for their duties, everyone sat backstage, whispering and watching the show. Nobody else had approached Chloe. She looked only to the screen, its gray image crackling, spasming and twisting away from its square frame as if bad weather tampered the signal. Other actors brushed past on their ways to the stage, and Chloe watched them transition from the physical backstage to whatever glitch hid in the television. And soon, the play neared its close.

So quickly had her first show finished! What could she do now but wait for the next play and its rounds of auditions? What would she think as she looked back at today, and what would Phoebe think? Chloe had started calling her Phoebe, removing her title. An urge to know her mother's opinion pricked at her, pulled at her; she needed to know, and as Chloe thought more about Phoebe, a woman tapping her daughter's head, tapping and saying anything about the play, Chloe constricted, nails digging into her sleeves. Would Phoebe like what she was doing (she was doing all she could, she appealed to an impressionist painting, a vague woman blending in blue), or

would she wish her in an acting role, something more presti-
gious?

Chloe had a headache. Her eyes grew black spindles and
webs. Uncertainty drove her nails deeper, farther down the
fabric. She would remember this day forever, yes she was sure
of it, and she would always remember how proud Phoebe
would've been, and there she sat!

The first row of the audience could be seen on screen,
and there sat Phoebe Barnett, shifting her attention from the
stage to the camera filming it, backstage to Chloe and beyond.
Here she appeared, and they looked at each other, mother
and daughter, and Chloe's breath caught and the webs spread
further over her vision, and her skin grew hot.

The lights died, and the scene vanished with them. The
swift dark swallowed Phoebe, but the final act was starting,
and before it could, the stagehands set to work. Chloe rose,
startled from the trance with her head still pounding as the
others hurried past. She took up the rear of the train and was
responsible for flipping the backdrop from Wonderland to a
quiet garden. It was a piece of painted muslin on a cardboard
frame the length of the stage, and Chloe grabbed the side with
both hands and pulled it backward, wheels spinning in their
regular circle until the scene was set again. She stood now at
the other end of the stage and realized that Phoebe should be in
front of her: the first row, just to the left. The other stagehands
finished their business and scurried back, but Chloe stood
breathless onstage and searched whatever faces she could for
the one she needed.

But she wasn't there. Her legs wobbled, and she scanned
faster, checked further into the dark, into people she couldn't
see but looked for anyway, and she wasn't there, and oh God
where did she go? A moment more, Chloe told herself, please

God one second more on stage, and keep the lights off a little longer. She was here. She was here. She had to be here.

Webs wrapped her vision, and the headache pumped hot toxins into her skull. Legs folded under her, and she lost consciousness.

THIS WAS THE STORY that filtered through Highland Winters in the few months before Chloe graduated. All reliable accounts related that Chloe Barnett fainted during the play, though few recounted that it happened while the lights were off, and nobody said that she was carried to the back before they returned. Nobody saw her pass out, and nobody knew about it but Pierre, who carried her back, and whoever else was backstage at the time. But by all accounts, Chloe fainted during the play, and consensus stated that it was a spectacle for anyone in the audience.

Chloe struggled to live beyond this gossip long after it ceased. She was never a household name, and few students went to the play to begin with, and as summer passed and life at Clearwater High started, only Chloe remembered the incident. She wasn't embarrassed anymore, but time hadn't set that night behind her.

As a freshman, she waited urgently for the next show. She signed up for Clearwater's *Introduction to Theater* class, and Mrs. Hemmings, its teacher, told her she had talent. Chloe enjoyed her teaching to the same degree Mrs. Hemmings enjoyed teaching her, and when the next play peaked on the horizon—Chloe's first in high school—Mrs. Hemmings let its title slip in their passing conversations. This was a level of privilege Chloe had never felt before, privilege beyond what she thought possible for herself. To rise to the top of her class and spar her talents with peers was something, but to rub shoulders with the teacher was an entryway to all future shows and perhaps post–high school opportunities. Her relationship with Mrs. Hemmings stood now as one of her most cherished bonds, second only to Phoebe, Henry, and Jane. She spent the rest of the school day researching the play in the library, and when Henry picked her up at the bell, she told him the news.

"What's it called?" he asked as he pulled out of the parking lot.

"*The Tempest.*"

He nodded. Chloe knew he didn't know what she was talking about, so she elaborated.

"It's a Shakespeare play. One of his last, Mrs. Hemmings said."

He smiled. "That old coot at it again?"

Chloe laughed, and Henry followed. They passed through town. The streets were still relatively quiet before Clearwater's students could walk them—nightlife was four hours out. Still, Chloe couldn't help but stare out the windows as she always did, and again she was dragged back to elementary school, imagining buildings as teeth, and reflexively, she rubbed over her own with her tongue.

"Mom'd be so proud of you, y'know."

"I might not get the part."

A new character in the teeth memory: Phoebe sat behind the wheel. The windows were down, and pop music sung through the cabin. Chloe wished she could say something to her, but whenever she turned from the window, Phoebe's eyes turned to the road, and her face was blank anyway, forgotten until Chloe looked again at her portrait hanging above the mantle. It was a self portrait painted by Phoebe years before she left, and a real picture of her rested in Henry's bedroom, a candid face on a speedboat while the hole of Glass Lake watched from the background.

At present, Chloe turned in her chair, and Henry replaced Phoebe's impression. The windows were up, and no music played in the car.

"She'd be proud," Henry said. "No matter what."

"I know," she said. But why hadn't he responded quicker? Landing the part was Chloe's chief priority now, and she thought it would be Phoebe's too. She didn't know how she could find Phoebe in the crowd again if she didn't act the starring role, or how Phoebe would receive her shortcomings. No, Chloe needed this part, and Henry's pause proved it. He knew Phoebe would only be proud when Chloe was proud, and his optimism only served to blunt her sure suspicions. She needed to wear Miranda.

Henry drove along the forest now, and as the conversation died, they hummed into the garage. Chloe used all her excess time that night watching any recordings she could of the play, thinking and plotting.

BEFORE SCHOOL STARTED, CHLOE stashed her backpack in its locker, taking only her *Introduction to Theater* binder. Few other students roamed the school this early, their numbers growing as the bell drew closer, so she hurried down the hall as fast as walking could take her. Mrs. Hemmings, Chloe knew from bumping into her often before school started, would arrive in around ten minutes. Down the stairs and around the library she went, past the cafeteria and through a wing beside the auditorium. Mrs. Hemmings's office was built into a wall here in the theater backrooms, and relief emptied into her to find the door unlocked. She whispered her thanks.

The room was no larger than a closet. A door of solid oak connected the office to the backstage, and to Chloe's right stood a column of filing cabinets. Mrs. Hemmings's desk was at the left, and Chloe started here, rifling through neat stacks of paper, sifting through folders. She found only forms, grades, and nothing in the drawers below. She turned to the filing cabinets and found in one a complete genealogy dating back thirty years of every show performed by the Clearwater High Players, all the way to the previous teacher. The first play was *Mary Poppins*, and she skimmed through to last year's production of *Our Town*. And before this now was another folder!

Footsteps in the hall.

Chloe opened it, found ample scripts for *The Tempest*, slipped one into her binder, closed the folder and the cabinet, and fled through the stage door as the echoes neared.

She caught herself onstage, safe now, panic clearing. Her breathing slowed. The only lights on at this hour were those at the front entrance where the seats ended. She looked at the empty rows before her and thought what they'd look like on opening day, all their admiring eyes. She imagined the brilliant stage lights revealing a new Chloe, someone else for a moment, an enchanted Miranda. In all her imaginings, a mannequin sat to the left; Chloe had long since forgotten what she looked like.

She did it for her. Yes, Chloe did it for her, and if she wasn't there in the front row, she wouldn't have done it. If she wasn't watching from somewhere out there, she never would have done it. It was bad, Chloe knew, taking that script, but it wasn't her fault, and if it was, this ghost outweighed all consequence. It was Phoebe's fault that she needed to reach higher. It was Phoebe's fault that she needed to make someone proud.

It was Phoebe whom Chloe saw in *Alice in Wonderland*, and it was Phoebe whom she searched for again during *The Tempest*.

She got the part. Mrs. Hemmings never suspected foul play, though she was short a script when handing them out properly three weeks later. Auditions passed Chloe with glowing marks, and after two months of rehearsals, the stage was set, and an audience filtered into their seats. Chloe was backstage with Pierre when the doors opened.

"How're you feeling?" Pierre asked. He was still a stagehand.

She crossed her arms. "Anxious."

"But you'll do great."

Chloe was sure she would. She had practiced as an addict ever since she pocketed the play, and her repetition left no chance for mistakes. Performance became a machine, something for which she needed only to activate and exceed all expectations. And Chloe hoped this machine would yield its product. She looked out from the right wing to the seats at the left of the audience. She scratched her arm.

She and Pierre talked a while longer before Mrs. Hemmings drew everyone together for her final encouraging remarks. Then, she walked onstage to welcome the crowd, and the group broke into actors and stagehands, and Chloe and Pierre parted. Chloe didn't much like being alone anymore. She recognized now that she thought a lot when she was alone, and she didn't always like where her thoughts ended. They turned to bitter whispers, always dwelled and dreaded on the past, melancholic.

But Chloe wasn't stuck inside today. She was a star, and until the curtains closed, she would function on practice alone, reserving no room for thoughts outside the show. She would curl the world to adoration and demonstrate to one woman who her daughter had become.

She waited mechanically for her entrances and exits and delivered her part as the maiden on a forgotten island. She performed with greater elegance than she had ever practiced, spoke and acted in complete sincerity, and all the while, her mind trained on other things, of her growing heartbeat and seat A3, an empty chair. Scenes and acts passed, and after each, Chloe sat backstage and didn't let herself think. A healthy television took the role of the middle school's static box, and Chloe watched it. Nothing strange happened, and the final act started, and the final scene with it.

Chloe stood resplendent now with her contemporaries in the play. She stood with her father and her lover, stood apart from the noblemen on stage right. Her line approached, and she scanned the crowd and A3 for any sign of anything.

"How many goodly creatures there are here!" she started. A pause: in Miranda's context, a pause of excitement, finding her next words. As Chloe, it bought time. Why hadn't she come? No one in the crowd was "goodly" save Henry in the back row! Nobody was worth the performance she practiced and maintained but the one woman who wasn't there, and had Chloe disappointed her? Was she enough, or was Chloe only a memory or fantasy to her, to Phoebe living in the mirror? Something inherent in Chloe could never amount to a noteworthy sum, something corporeal, something cheap and insipid, something disconnected from infinity and all those who came and died before her. She tread waters of herself and obscurity, for Phoebe was gone, Phoebe had sunk, Phoebe had given herself to the world of thoughts.

Chloe wanted to drown. She thought about drowning or crashing or swallowing or a lot of things after this play, all through high school. She would cry some nights, scream some nights, revolt at herself and the absent ghost and wait, but no one appeared at the window, no one stood stark against her portrait. She stopped thinking about drowning or crashing or swallowing the night she talked with Jane on the dock.

In this moment in the play, she moved forward. "O brave new world that has such people in it!" No more lines were left to recite. Phoebe hadn't come, and Chloe felt so very small in noxious skin and stringy hair. Another line, another phrase would've cut and crumbled her into shrapnel scattered onstage. But she propped herself with something ambiguous, universal, a feeling that she had finished something, and soon, the lights cut out, and Chloe walked backstage thinking it's over, it's over.

# 13

Chloe didn't know her mother died, only that she disappeared and her father talked to himself. His voice trailed to her loft and woke her early on Saturday.

"She's not with you?" he said to someone below. "Jesus, I just don't get it. I'll call you back." A pause. "Hey, have you seen Phoebe? No, I don't. I don't know. I'm scared, Noel." This was Jane's mother and a good friend of Phoebe's. She told Henry that they had been together earlier that week, spent time shopping and eating together, but that was all.

"I don't know" was the only thing Henry said between phone calls, the only thing he could say while the ringer chimed. He repeated it in a harsh, quick warble.

This was the only evidence for Phoebe's absence: a slip of paper torn from a notebook reading, *I don't know*. Henry woke to it on the kitchen counter, and hysterics followed when she wasn't found in the house, deepened as unanswered texts aged, unanswered calls to Phoebe and whatever god was around. He grabbed the paper and took it with him as he made coffee, as he searched the house, as he called for her, as he called.

"Talk to her recently?" he was asking. Henry didn't want to look at the paper, but he did so every few minutes to reassure that the words hadn't changed. And every time he did, its epitaph repeated with cyclical dread, increasing and involuntary fear; his mind grasped at whatever it could to stop its foundering, and now it only grasped at a woman's memory, and he didn't know why she left, and he didn't know what she didn't know. He was green and starved; he was nature torn at its folds; he was scraps of a house undone. And the routine of everything, with this fissure in its fabric, could never exist again. No longer would he wake the same or make the same coffee or raise their same daughter. Twenty years with Phoebe faded, would fade, would be forgotten or forced to be forgotten. He could never remember her without this day, and as these hours irrevocably changed their relationship, he needed to forget—he wanted to forget. Or he shouldn't forget—I don't know, he thought.

"She's gone," he said, crying now. Sobbing, Chloe thought, but she didn't like that word. He kept his voice down, but everything reeked through thin floorboards and wallpaper, and now certainty struck her that she would never see her mother again.

"No, she's really gone." Now she heard the man below convincing himself, finalizing it and stuffing it in the closet to gather dust, to discard. And with his conviction, Chloe understood she wouldn't see her again, at least not, she told herself—in the same sidestep of her father's forgetfulness, an elusion of the animate shadow of grief seeking to trail them both—for a very long time. But all things ended after a very long time, and this too would pass one day like a loud dream, tortuous for a sleeping breath but buried and unrecalled every moment after.

Chloe was right about this in one way: she would remember almost none of this day and only fragments of the coming years. In high school, a science class would take a stint into psychology, and in this class she would wonder, the woman she was, whether she would have remembered more from her Early Development (as the textbook termed it) if Phoebe never left, or if Chloe hadn't been awake and listening to her father's groans. Would she have remembered more had there been anything to remember but listlessness, days where the oppressive sun stood too high and she too low, or the moon too still and she shaking, falling apart, scrabbling to be anyone else? She felt hardly alive then and saw herself as a machine, as a chunk of skin and joints, an observer apart from the world. Would she have remembered more were she not a machine then, or were these pasts always designed to rot and, as seaborn rock is scratched by a tide, to erode, to fall away, to return to something beyond? Chloe looked up to the teacher now, a man who led the discussion toward mental illness and its causes. Phoebe dusted all her memories with a patina of static. That was all she would remember in all her senses from the day Phoebe died: the taste and gravity of a lake above her.

"I don't know."

She stood from bed and felt the machinery in her for the first time. She checked her phone. Jane had asked her an hour ago if she wanted to go swimming with her and "the others," as she called them, though Chloe didn't know them well enough yet to staple herself to the group. She only vaguely knew who Jane referenced. They had gone swimming a month ago, and though she knew their names then, she was already losing the past. Waves climbed the shore.

*Yes,* she sent back.

*The lake alright?* The reply was immediate.

*Yes.*

Jane told her to meet them at five.

The machine walked her downstairs. Henry wasn't in the kitchen anymore. He retreated to his study where he would sit all day, and when Chloe came home that evening, he would confirm that Phoebe wouldn't come back.

Chloe always asked him (always had to ask him) to hang out with friends when the option presented itself, but she didn't ask today, and Henry never questioned her where she went.

She sat on the couch now and turned on the television to a high school drama. Episodes played on repeat, and Chloe watched them until the sun started down again and Jane knocked. Chloe left the show on as she answered the door, as she changed into her bathing suit, as she left down the sidewalk. Jane was talking to her, and she was talking back, but she couldn't recall anything that was said. Questions and statements were listened to, replied to, and gone, and how much nicer Jane looked than she with thin lips, she with stringy arms and hair like dried, splitting wheat, how Jane's body was strung together with cords of flesh and pillars of bone, and how Chloe's was a thing dismantling and reconstructing, indefinite. She thought back to their sleepover two years ago and the girl she saw in her reflection, rubbing her arms now and feeling the bones again, thankful they hadn't shrunk or shriveled and dreading they would fall out. Chloe knew she would die as she took another breath or another step, and the filament inside would snap, and surgeons would recover her arms and diagnose them remarkably long, would rub the skin of her legs and term a new color for it.

She remembered also from the sleepover the image of Phoebe in the dining room, Phoebe with a salad, but the floor, the fridge, and the woman had started melting into their base colors and shapes. Phoebe's eyes and clothes were lost in abstraction, and her body became a tan oblong. Only her lips remained distinct as a dripping crescent moon.

Here was the forest: a darkening web of hanging branches and hung leaves. Where it once gave and took in the wind, its boughs stuck now in sharp angles and drained all sound and color from the woods, caught all wind in gossamer sieves and leafy nets. Jane led Chloe on the footpath, stumbling over roots and downcast arms (how these sticks looked like arms, Chloe thought, like broken joints and cracked arms), and something above Chloe buckled her legs, tripped her on a rock, dropped her to her hands. Jane asked if she was okay, and she said she was and it was okay and everything was okay, but something held her down as she stood and trudged on, and she concealed the effort of walking with this extra labor, a heightened pressure. She thought it was the heat, but the woods were cool—not cool, but nothing, neither hot nor cold nor any degree to either side. So it was hunger, then; she hadn't eaten anything yet, and she asked Jane what time it was.

"Five thirty," she said. "Ish. They'll be waiting on us."

But her stomach stopped aching hours ago, and now she was only weak, fatigued. Something else wanted to ground her in the dirt, to pin her in brambles and drag her head along the moss. Something else wanted to lose her in the woods, but the machine carried her as the girls neared the lake.

In Chloe's psychology unit, the teacher would spend part of a lecture talking about "auto-piloting," or forgetting one is alive while his body works without him. This was Chloe's machine, and she recognized it as being "stuck inside." The teacher explained that while the body performed its menial tasks, the brain functioned in its train of thought, working overtime to think, and that was all.

In the forest, Chloe's body and brain furthered their separation. Some thoughts slipped through, but she knew she couldn't handle them right now, looming things, precocious things, couldn't handle the wall's collapse and the flood, the intake, out from her eyes and mouth, and where was she and oh, she was slipping—

She patched the leak.

Glass Lake widened before them. Mallory and Pierre threw sticks at each other on shore, but Chloe still couldn't remember their names, and for fear of breaking the dam, she didn't wonder, didn't ask. The little row boat was still buoyed to the dock, everything golden, nothing in disrepair. The lake harbored quiet waters, and a flock of birds somewhere near took to song, to droning, strident notes. Trees halted at the shore to form a vague frame around the sky with its clouds, and just below the frame's center, the sun burned on, and Chloe heaved forward.

"Are you alright?" Jane asked before they breached the treeline and privacy dissolved.

Chloe didn't hear her. "Alright," she said, walking out.

The boys welcomed her and Jane as she followed, explaining their pirate duel. They pointed to the boat now and said they wanted to go sailing. Jane talked to them, and Chloe's eyes followed the boys' intention, lighting on a girl laying in the boat (hiding, thought Chloe). She walked along the dock to inspect her. The girl wore dark, pinned hair and pink sunglasses, pink nails, and even outside the halls Chloe recognized her as Sylvia Stockton, a loud girl and Mallory's girlfriend, a brief friend in elementary school, though neither of them mentioned that history, their futures diverging. She looked sour, and Chloe was repulsed to look at her, though not in the same wind as her bitterness for Mrs. Lavine. Sylvia was of a different breed, she knew, someone so far removed from their group, from any group, that everyone was amazed she stayed with Mallory as long as she did, that now Chloe looked at her not as a person but a character. Chloe hated that she was a character so concrete, a girl unchanged by the tides. Who Sylvia was in truth didn't matter for Chloe to distance herself, only that she knew the clarity and definition with which Sylvia lived, and the knowledge of her own finite self led Chloe to ask, "Who are you?"

Sylvia may have looked at her behind her lenses, but she didn't move. "Bored."

And hunger hit once as a drill in Chloe's stomach.

"Hungry?"

"No" was the stopped answer. "Um."

And the others filtered past her and brushed arms to climb the boat. They all wore swimsuits exposing pale skin save Sylvia who wore jean shorts and a T-shirt, Sylvia with a tan body, another trait keeping her out of Chloe's portrait of normalcy. She had grown before any of the other girls, looked nicer and dressed nicer and everything had its proportion in her, this woman. Chloe looked down at her own body and her heart quickened, panicked, and she would evaporate soon, become ethereal, watch the skin flicker—

But they all waited on the boat, and Chloe joined them. Mallory sat at the front, Pierre at the rear, and Chloe and Sylvia on the middle plank. Jane sat on the floor between them. The boys paddled with difficulty out on the lake, still discussing their pirate conflicts, and Jane joined them now, but the woman and the girl at the center were silent and still. Chloe looked to the forest, now distant enough on all sides for details to blend in the same way the image of Phoebe shaped and colored into itself as her boat of eleven years, this scarecrow of hers, drove and rattled with the minute hand, the hour hand, the passing of days. At the center of the lake, the woods became a dark and shapeless mass as would appear in a dream, as did appear in many dreams after, from which Chloe would wake and bite her inner lip and think I'm here, I'm still here.

The kids said things about Glass Lake. Mallory told her (that was his name, the boy at the front with dinosaurs on his swim trunks) all the things they said about it in elementary school, the murders and the monsters and everything just behind the water's veil and the reeds' sanctuary. This loud "they," the faces around her, folk like Sylvia of solid stock, were those who held it together and told stories of those who didn't. The murdered all sank, they said, and with time, the murderers would follow. And all that lived beyond reason lived also below the surface, lived outside of life, and whatever that was, Chloe didn't want to recognize. Dinosaurs and dogmen and all the fairy tale demons were somewhere here, and Chloe looked in the water.

It was the kind of blue that a blizzard turned the evening sky, the kind that loaded clouds were tinted when storming miles away, days away. The water turned black some feet below the surface, its border marked by a lone fish, a small fish so deep, hovering where light could only brush and make a shadow of the swimmer. But the water rippled, erupted, and the boat shook, and the fish fled. Her friends had jumped; her friends hung now with swinging legs at the surface, rippling into each other, shouting something or other. The fish had gone, and in its place were the shaking reflections of trees, of blocky oaks and willows, and just to her left was printed a shimmering sun.

And here was the moon behind it, at Chloe's antipode or beneath it, somewhere under the earth. She grew tall with this under-moon, tall knowing the sun wouldn't rise for a few hours more. She had conquered it all and was alive. Something beat in her chest, pushed out her chest, in again, out. The starboard abraded her hands as she gripped the edge and leaned over the moon or its reflection in the pool, cursing in her mind, cursing at something she couldn't grasp, shouting a name. But the name was cold already, and Chloe asked the moon where she went, where she herself would go, but it only flickered in the waves, and the swimmers kept their tumult. The boat rocked. And what happens when we run out? Chloe asked the moon, What happens when my teeth drop and my skin turns to sand, my bones to shells, and I crack, I sunder where I stand? (I will crack, will sunder any minute. At any time and for any reason I will unwind, leave, be remembered and forgotten.) I am a bag of broken bones, she thought. I am litter, daughter and waste, with too many thoughts, and was there anything behind the moon? But someone was there before it, someone where the fish once hovered. It was human, then woman, then she was there! She swam too deep, only a face in the water, but she called to her, Chloe knew she was calling to her, but sound wouldn't break the surface. Ripples tore the image again, and sprays from the pirates were buckshot scattering Phoebe's features in bloodless gore. Chloe had to save her, or she had to be with her, if only for a moment. And she leaned further and fell, sucking a short breath before lungs hit water, before she started her descent.

Glass Lake was warm but chilled as she sank. Feet kicked around Chloe like seaweed on the roof, but these rose past as she drifted down the oubliette. Sunlight stabbed beams into the water, and these left after the legs. Everything became shadow, then too dark for shadows. The ocean was loud, but waves and screams muddied themselves in shifting currents, streams running up one ear and past the other, rivers of bubbling wind as if in some primordial cauldron. The night sky filled her vision, but no stars hung there. It was empty. Chloe hadn't moved since her departure, and now a fish swam to her, bit her arm, and fled, this lone star. Chloe spread her arms and felt them tingle and fade.

They said a talking fish named Nimbus lived here. He appeared in the deep now, crept out of nothing, and returned as the body fell past. His scales were on fire and diamonds supplanted his eyes, and he seemed to say a lot to Chloe, but she didn't hear.

Her vision blurred and threatened to expire. A lot of things lived here, they said, all of whom were beyond this world, but nothing more crossed her path. The stories were wrong or only excerpts of truth. Nothing lived beneath this world, no great ghosts, no reunions, no goodbyes or forevers. No one could see her go. She liked this privacy, needed it. She couldn't bear anyone watching her go, couldn't carry the weight of eyes. (She was embarrassed, she knew, embarrassed of all this.) What would they say at school? Chloe Barnett drowned in the lake, Chloe Barnett drowned with her mother, Chloe Barnett's arms washed ashore, Chloe Barnett's gone, gone. She unspooled now, drifted apart, one line of static in a broken system. This was the lake, and this was death: floating against gravity, defying pressure, driftwood stuck in the stream.

A face appeared inches before her, and only a face, the rest falling quickly in the void. It's Phoebe, she thought through the fuzz; it's mom, she knew. But where were her eyes, and where was her mouth? A blank woman, a smooth woman, a woman Chloe couldn't decipher with scrapped eyes, but yes, it was Phoebe! So there were reunions—

But Chloe jerked upward, her body caving at the back, and the woman returned to the water and night, and Chloe ascended, the lake unclouding, blueing, light returning. Nimbus had left, but she and all her senses still fell to a numbness, a throbbing, a scraping treble.

The lake left her, and she was dragged to the boat and laid in its hull. She gasped for air, drank it hysterically, vomiting water and bile, shivering in a pool of spit. As she breathed, the effects of the lake softened, and her vision cleared to the others crowding over her. Mallory hunched directly behind, blocking the sun. Pierre and Jane sat to her right, and Pierre was saying, "Good job" to her, saying "She's back, she's here."

Mallory stared. His eyes lit with admiration or wonder, and the woman at the rear, the clothed woman, watched the commotion with interest and nothing more, maybe relieved, but nothing belied it. She didn't speak, didn't move. Had she seen Chloe's fall and still sat idly? Chloe was ashamed that these eyes might have followed her, that these eyes and no others would've watched her go, that someone with such a place in the world, such a role and function as anyone else at Highland Winters, would've been her lone witness. But Phoebe watched too, and now she was trapped with the former and without the latter, and as Chloe drew clear breaths, she saw the woman tighten again and disengage as Chloe puked.

"Say something!" Pierre commanded this twice before, but Chloe only registered it as she lapsed outside herself. "Are you okay?"

No answer would resolve the day, and no answer could cover it, communicate it, anyway. "Hungry," she said, and she was. Her bile was empty.

Mallory dug around the helm of the boat and unlatched a small tackle box nailed to the floor. (This would be the first to disappear after the boat ran aground, stuck in soil, vandalized by boys and nature.) He pulled out and handed her a granola bar which she held in frail hands. She fumbled unwrapping it while the others prodded.

"Did you see the bottom?" Pierre asked.

She shook her head. Or nodded, maybe, but some motion was apparent.

"Did you see anything cool?"

Mallory started rowing back, and Chloe took her first vitalizing bites, recalling the hunger that seemed so primal on any day but this. She was glad her mouth was full now, but it didn't stop memories (memories already filed away) of the descent and nadir, Phoebe Barnett or something else as outline only, skin only. As they ferried away from the lake's center, trees from the opposite shore covered the sun, and everything turned a shade of bronze. The world was still a haze to Chloe as she dismounted the boat, touched grass again, stood by while the others collected their things. This haze would smother her years before and after the day Phoebe left, and when she tried to recall anything from these years, nothing would return. She thought now, walking through the woods with her friends, that she had died. The granola bar ran out, but still she had no answers to the questions posed to her, questions the haze wouldn't give passage to. So when it was time to go, when they reached the end of the forest and the start of the world, they went their separate ways. Jane hugged her and said something short and sweet, and Chloe smiled, and they left each other.

No one else filled the sidewalk on Chloe's walk home, a straight line along the forest. It was only a minute away. Bugs drummed their shrill, vociferous screen over the forest whose trees still hung limp and rigid. It was almost something to cry at, but footsteps came fast behind, and Mallory joined her, out of breath.

"Had to say goodbye to Sylvia," he panted. "But wanted to make sure you're okay."

She glanced at him, glanced back home, said, "Okay" not from recognition but mimicry.

"So, I don't know," he started. But he looked good in this light, Chloe thought, and she knew she shouldn't think it, but the haze cleared for a moment in the spell. "I mean," he said, "last time we were here, we talked about all the stories kids used to say about that place. Do you think, um." He looked handsome, beautiful, but cobbled like her. "Do you think, now that you've been there—*there* there, I mean—that any of them are real?"

They crossed the street to her house, and she didn't think about what she said until after it left her mouth and she lay cradling herself in bed. "Some of them are."

And she left him on the sidewalk.

# 14

Mallory fled on the same sidewalk the night of Chloe's debut in *Hamlet*. It was also the sidewalk that, in a few hours, Jane would find Cecil stumbling onto, Cecil collecting dirt and bruises, raving about no one and nothing. Mallory passed this spot now, and streetlights fizzed to life in wide sprays of light, concentrating, hardening into cones. He turned in one of these cones to search the edges of the night behind.

He wasn't following.

Mallory didn't have time to think about Cecil's confrontation; the play would start in ten minutes. So he ran, and Pierre followed Cecil, and somewhere in the dark was the bar they had met at. It all seemed unreal, seemed that someone else lived in Mallory's body and played out the past minutes without him, just as someone else played Cecil's part and Pierre's. This perception and the encounter that instilled it were two phenomena Mallory had never experienced before, so that at twenty-one years of age, he felt for the first time not himself. The sentiment eroded the walls of his mind, ate at the barrier, and he wanted more than his life to return to the world as it was ten minutes ago, an hour ago, to never have gone to the bar, to never inherit this otherness.

And the otherness was double: the feeling itself, a stranger in his body, but deeper, its root, the sudden wailing from a spot unknown, the realization that he lost something impor-tant—not unknown, rather, but underdeveloped. This was the same plague of the younger Mallory arriving home alone, microwaving his dinner in a closeted dark. But that wound was subterranean, a hole bored steadily, all coming to light in the present. A waterfall cleaved deeper its bed, striking now a cave and flooding it; an ocean collapsed on Mallory. He wanted nothing but to vanish, perhaps to return when everything blew over. He was not untouchable but far too affectable, far too stricken by the whims of the hour, of whomever imposed their vices upon him, and he wanted only to beat nature to its purpose and disappear before anything turned to further grief. It was, he thought, the only action provided to him. Disappearing—or its synonym, which Mallory couldn't ad-mit—was all that nature afforded against itself. But now, he only had the courage to stand from the table, silent, and run.

He would disappear someday, he knew, and it appealed to him now as it did to everyone: not in words but adrenaline, to a soul charmed with hormones. Its appeal was birdsong, the chant of trees in the wind, and always the clatter of bugs. The continuity of the world was interrupted by every stopped heart, a fabric riddled with needles, and everything now cen-tered on the past, was built upon it. Everything to Mallory (scanning again for Cecil, finding no one, hurrying to the theater) was mortal, a reminder. But something was still to be gained, to patch and fill his torn seams. Chloe waited at the Vintage, and she would fill, at least in part, some need. She would wind the clock back before anything but them together, them alone somewhere, fixed. Anything that walked the streets or lived in childhood rumors was unreliable. Ghosts could no longer reach the boy now as he rounded the corner and came upon Chloe's life.

The marquee was a fire, and neon smoked in the hearth. The night sky was tall and thick, and lamps endured as Atlas to support a black ocean. Jane stood by the ticket booth and caught Mallory's eyes across the street. She smiled but frowned as he approached.

She noticed his cheek. "What happened?"

His eyes welled now. Tears collected as a burden in his speech. "Did you get the tickets?"

She handed him his slip, and they walked inside. Jane waited for concessions, and Mallory waited for her. The Vintage was dustier than he remembered, but the thin waft of cleaning supplies still fogged the air. "Where are the others?" she asked.

"They'll be late." He forced it out, looking through the auditorium doors, and the stage lights were off, were gone.

"And the bruise?"

Mallory touched his face and stung himself.

She lowered her voice. "What happened?"

Any answer would betray Cecil or himself, but prolonged silence contrived an answer and made lying impossible. "Cecil hit me," he admitted, and relief filled him. She was his confidant now.

Her eyes were troubled waters. "I'm sorry. He—I should've told you."

"Um."

"He's high energy sometimes, when he's frustrated. It's no excuse, but Jesus, I should've told you guys." Her upper half folded above crossed arms as if she would puke.

"That he gets violent?" he whispered.

Jane bought her popcorn and clutched the lip of the bag. She led him to a corner. "Yes, so." She stopped and started, started and stopped. "He killed Sylvia, or maybe he didn't, we don't know."

His thoughts jammed suddenly with scenes from the bar, scenes approximating a murderer. Mallory coughed. "What?"

"We don't know for sure. I know, he just, I don't know, takes things out of proportion. Is he alright now?"

Proportion: Mallory saw in his rememberings a bloodied specter, a charged, haunting air. But now any tears coming flamed to alarm. "I don't know what he's doing, or Pierre."

"It's not that I don't trust him, but are they together?"

Pierre followed Cecil from the bar, but had he found him, and what would happen if he did? "I don't know, maybe." But Mallory knew he'd found him. They were talking or fighting now, but he couldn't be sure, he couldn't be sure.

"God." She shook her head. Mallory found a surprising kinship between them as they huddled together and shed secrets. They were never particularly close, but now they fostered a kind of conspiracy, as if the crisis formed an odd intimacy. He stood elated and suspended above the events of that night, watching the town with new profundity in this friendship. It was almost worth it just for this. So when Jane suggested they forget it all till tomorrow, they could just deal with it all tomorrow, Mallory agreed, turned once more to check the doors, and prayed to something that it would all work out, wherever they were. Then he removed himself from that life and followed Jane to their seats.

The crowd lights were on but dim, stuffed into small mouths in the ceiling. Most seats were taken, but as they neared the stage, an empty pocket revealed itself. "Front row?" she asked. "To see your girl?"

"Yeah, that's good." He noticed a disconnect between his voice and his mind, and everything he said was cautious. His words plumbed a dark room. "My girl."

They sat to the left, and a bottomless frenzy set upon them both. Everything about that night and Cecil lay before them, as did each other's awareness of the evidence and its dangers. Anything could happen to Pierre, to Cecil, to anyone, but neither of the showgoers needed to believe it. Jane never thought Cecil killed her to begin with, and only on his insistence to take him seriously had she caved. But she expected nothing more to come from this night than typical melodrama. Mallory held no such pretensions and still believed terrible things would come, but this was an escape: these seats, this show, and Chloe above it all. He would see her, and everything would be well. But still all this knowledge loomed too large to ignore but larger still to apprehend.

"Hm?" She was looking at him, telling him with her eyes to keep that thing between them small and quiet.

"What?"

"You sound scared."

"Oh," he said. "It's not official yet."

Jane set the popcorn between them and started in. "What do you mean 'official?'"

Air pressed on Mallory, restrained him, fettered his lungs. "It just doesn't feel right, I guess."

"To you?"

But there was a murder. Red prints tracked the walls. "To, um."

"You can have some if you want." She nudged the bag to him.

"To her." He took a kernel and placed it on his tongue. It was bitter, metallic, but he swallowed. He looked to the stage and imagined her there, and how much would lift from him when she came? "To Chloe," he repeated.

"Ah." But the lights dimmed, and the crowd found their seats. Jane saved two beside her in a contingency neither of them expected, but maybe they would come late. "It's okay," Jane whispered, closing her phone. "There's always tomorrow."

"Tomorrow." He didn't recognize it.

"Always."

The lights faded, and a suited man walked into a spotlight. He introduced the show, but Mallory couldn't hear. He was stuck inside, he knew, but no exit made itself apparent; rather, he wanted to stay inside. No, he didn't want to but needed to; there was more to process of Cecil, more packets of time to unwrap and examine, the requirement to understand this man and slot him into any pattern of life saved in Mallory's brain, to file him away and forget it all to normalcy. But this was a thing too boundless in size or complexity to file, something setting itself outside Mallory's life, haunting him now with the added phantom of his parents' absence, another incalculable heap. But still he focused; still he reasoned. Still this murder and Cecil's exit that night wisped around reason.

The actors were here, a boy and his father's ghost standing on a parapet over a field of fog.

The boy was a pillar, alone, thinking, talking, exiting stage right.

A woman glowed to the left in a white dress, hair knotted in a crown. It was Chloe and Ophelia. And now Mallory stopped thinking and couldn't imagine ever having thought at all. She was here. She was eternal, and all his thoughts transient.

Another man entered from the corner. "Fear it, my dear sister," he said, "and keep you in the rear of your affection, out of the shot and danger of desire."

She was beautiful. And she was solid, filed squarely into life, lived experiences past and present. She was Mallory entire, but as the actor spoke his line, something shifted deep in her bones, revealing itself in a fragile frown. Her eyes flicked for a moment then to Mallory and Jane or past them. She would've smiled, Mallory thought, had she seen them. But she was back to the play with a placid complexion, engaged in conversation. It was such a quick, imperceptible break in character that Mallory wondered if it happened at all, or if he was still stuck thinking, imagining what he wanted to see.

Chloe said, "I shall the effect of this good lesson keep as watchmen to my heart."

THE NIGHT BEFORE, CECIL started his car. Conscience told him to leave earlier, and he would be late now, and why was he always late? The party was at seven, and the clock's red numbers read the same. He would be ten minutes late or five if he cut through town, potential traffic. The car pulled from his apartment's lot and turned toward the main roads. Cecil wore a denim jacket and joggers, both reeking of dryer sheets, mementos of spilled liquor. A finger strayed a moment above his phone on the console—should he text them, text Jane he would be late? But it would only be five minutes, and he brought the finger back to its place on the wheel, and the other hand rolled open the window.

White cocoons shot from the headlights, illuminating the world as it passed: sidewalks and the rats in their cracks, faces plastered in door frames and windows, lamps and streetlights dead and wavering. All fell past, and the road kept its pace, always kept within the headlights' reach. October breathed a taciturn chill. People smoked and stared. The only buildings still alive at that time were bars and laundromats and underground services hidden in their folds.

Cecil wasn't happy to live so far in town, so far in what would be a larger city's economic divide. He had the money too, but when he thought about moving, shocks bit his brain and shivered through the skeleton, and that was the only counterargument needed. He could never think on it in greater depth than the initial question without the jittering, the flickering, the resolution to his current lot. And every few weeks, he would drink, and he knew these were connected—the stains on his shirts and the house key dangling now from the ignition—but the shocks could never be maintained, and neither could the consistent remembrances that the shocks would return, the doldrums of waiting for them, his settlement in this part of town and not with the people who knew what they were doing. Everyone else had names and faces and lives, their own and those affected. Everyone else was firm.

But the others kept him steady. A photo of them all together bobbed from the mirror. Prom's lights froze in the frame, and skeins of pink and lime smoke tinted their faces and the deafening black background. They held each other's shoulders in a line, and at one end, Mallory smiled, eyes closed. Chloe stood shorter beside him, but her expression was empty, just the crease of a smile below sagging eyes, each negating the other. Pierre was next, the tallest, another smiler, then Jane in a jumpsuit leaning forward and tipping the group with her. And Cecil closed the circuit, a bowl of snacks in his free hand and a red suit over his dress shirt. He looked exhausted, Cecil thought now. He looked tired. But the girl, the woman, who brought him to these friends was absent, or she was somewhere watching.

Cecil turned onto a side street now, a one-way no wider than an alley. Sidewalks thinned and crowded with trash cans and boxes, and nothing was awake. He turned on his brights, but she already fell against the hood, thudding against the bumper. A fountain of blond hair and glass shards broke against the windshield, and Cecil screamed the car to a halt. A dog barked.

He flung his door open and fixed a leg outside. "Oh god, are you okay?"

Nothing.

He reached across the hood and nudged her alive. She arched her back and receded from the car like a tide. Cecil saw now that the shattered glass wasn't the windshield's but the bottle's in the woman's hand, now only a jagged stump. "Are you hurt?" he asked again.

She leaned against a wall and rasped, "Oh, this is rich."

And through a matted wall of hair lived memory, lived spite, all dust-gray and untouched, unaccounted for at this place at this time; a growing piece of antiquity falling, bursting from her spot on the shelf, catching fire and relighting every fossil of their shared history until the museum bellowed in flames, collapsed, and buried Cecil. He spoke now as a ghost. "Sylvia?"

She mumbled.

"Are you hurt?"

White knuckles clutched the neck of her bottle stump. Her voice was a child's quiet wonder. "You're back for me."

He hadn't harmed her to any notable degree, Cecil made sure to note as she swayed against a building's plaster. She stood fine, if propped. "You're okay?"

"Fuck you." And wonder left.

He stammered, and now civility left too. "No, I'm not 'back for you.' Why are you even here?" But he knew the answer by the bottle, and she seemed to know everything, everything about Cecil Monroe, the secrets and doubts built in a year of friendship, ready now for their graves to open.

"Why are *you* here?" Her speech blended.

"Going to some friends." But why was he scared? Why did his standing leg quiver, and what fears hid in the cavities of his words?

She laughed once, a lone cackle in chorus with the barking dog. "Friends."

"Good friends," he assured her, he assured himself.

She raised the bottle and drank the air.

"I'm going, then." But he couldn't step back in the car. Something pulled him forward. The museum fire ate the air around him, and a breeze drafted from behind.

"Does it all suck shit yet?"

This wasn't the time, but he couldn't isolate himself. Maybe some small artery inside still hoped for things to be made right between them. Maybe she could come back, and he could forget this night ever happened, purge prom from history and live unburdened, censoring war from the archive. It was a selfless act. Or he was simply curious where all this would lead, and in any case, he trembled at the threshold of his car and the world, his friends and hot breath, the present and the past. "I'm fine," he said.

"Fine?" A crescendo, calming now, a murmur. "You're nothing."

He shook his head. "High school is over. Go home."

But she stepped forward with great strain. She fell against the hood again, and Cecil could do nothing but trail her with his eyes, paralyzed.

"You're not shit without them," she crooned.

"I'm leaving now." He found the resolve, a bead of opportunity in a downpour, to sit back in the car and close the door. Still she crawled up the hood, crawled as a cat in the underbrush. Cecil's breath quickened, but still he couldn't move, and when she made it to the glass, he tried unsuccessfully to brush her off with the wipers.

"Get off. Please," he said, "please."

She tapped at him. The bottle had cut her finger, and blood stamped itself to the windshield, now running thicker from the wound, a trail, two trails down the front, a series of rivers in crimson slits. "Just Cecil-fucking-Monroe, just a name. All you are." She trailed off and rubbed her bleeding finger on the windshield, trying to clean it.

"Just go. Just go." He started rolling up the driver's side window now, but Sylvia caught it with her free hand. All Cecil's strength left him, and the window wouldn't close, or he wouldn't close it. He was weak; he was small. He had to go.

"You're just everybody's friend, huh? Think you're so cool." She coughed, hacked. "But you're nobody without them. Bad artist. Flunked drunk." She pressed a clean finger on the inside of his window now, and her body spread against the windshield.

"Goodbye," Cecil announced, wavered.

She coughed, gagged. "Back soon."

She was hollow, faceless, and Cecil's reflection trembled next to her in the glass. Already he knew she was right, dreaded she was right. Cecil blinked his brights as a final warning, and Sylvia appeared as the nightmare shadow of a mouse on the wall, a nauseating dominance over his vision, his thoughts, clawing at identity.

"I'll... see you around." Again the wonder, or perhaps a distance between her words and malice. Her lowered gaze found its way through her hair, and deep caves cut under green eyes. She was asking a question.

But another bead of courage found Cecil in the storm, and his foot slammed the gas. Tires shrieked. The engine howled, and Sylvia's face flung from the windshield, her eyes printing themselves a moment longer in place. And her body followed and floundered over the front, tumbled on the roof, and crashed, broken, to the street. He rolled up the window and looked in the mirror as the town sped past again. A woman lay motionless in the road, and that bundle of tubes and bones and skin was the last he saw of her. His heart beat faster, and his breathing followed, panicking. He found the bottom of himself. Blood still streaked the windshield, and he set the wipers to a frenzy, a macabre metronome.

Don't think about it, he thought. Don't think.


THE FOREST WAS ROTTING, or the ground was wet. Pierre ran through brush and bough, and dirt sponged each step, and mud latched to his shoes. But Cecil was fast, and Pierre ran in his wake. He was somewhere here, somewhere in the dark—just don't lose him. A phone bobbed in his hand, its flashlight on but swallowed in the forest's starving night. He shoved loose branches back moments before they connected with his eyes, and he stopped every few steps as a foot caught on roots or sunk too deep in the autumn mire. He put the light up now, but not a glimmer of the man he chased was apparent. Not even the sounds of his steps on the brush cracked the air. Only the storm of bugs and the footprints before him were left, the former screaming at the latter, at Cecil somewhere ahead and at Pierre lagging. The bugs clouded the flashlight and crawled on Pierre's arm, and, cringing, he shook them off and ran.

But the air was familiar now, a breeze, a gust, and before Pierre now was a break in the arresting dark, a spot of light swelling in the trees' negative space, and as he broke past the tree line, he almost fell into the water.

He caught himself on a lip of the lake he had never explored before. Far to the western shore spread their usual stomping ground, painted only in meager moonlight glancing off the water's surface. To the east glowed the town's official dock, and a speedboat idled in its shallows. Sometimes a holler reached Pierre, sometimes a bar of pop music. But still these insects broke the music and the cheers in ravenous white noise, and still this lake, glossed with a field of stars and moon, flowed undisturbed by the boat's idling.

Pierre startled as his eye caught something in its corner. He looked again, and his heart calmed. Cecil sat at the edge of the lake, though small against the world and sliding closer to the brink. But before he could fall, Pierre lunged and grabbed the neck of his shirt, raising him back to land and laying him between a tree's tangled veins.

Pierre was hot and shaking. He stood above the crumpled man, yelling, "What's wrong with you?"

He didn't move. His shirt was torn along its side, and his jeans were needled with thorns and burs.

"Cecil." A command.

He rolled onto his back, and a stench rolled with him and turned Pierre away. Cecil's front was damp and crusted in spit and alcohol. "Who do"—he coughed—"d'you think you are?"

"You hit him! God, Cecil, what—" he couldn't finish, and now he paced around the shore.

"What have I done?" His voice was water. "What…"

"Yes, Cecil, what *have* you done?"

Another fit of phlegm. "What I had to. I swear, I swear."

"You didn't have to do anything." He took a breath and calmed to a vicious whisper. "You didn't need anything."

"It was me or her." He was crying now. "Me or her."

"What are you talking about?"

"She's crazy. She's—she was crazy."

And Pierre's head cleared some, and his body cooled. He couldn't forgive yet, but anger subdued to disappointment, to confusion. "Who is 'she?'"

"Nobody."

"What?"

"I'm nobody."

Pierre gripped his head in his hands and crouched next to the noxious wreck. "You're Cecil," he barked.

"Just a friend," he said. "No one else."

"What?"

"You too." He hadn't looked at him since the bar, but now he turned an inspecting gaze over his hunched form, his hung head. "You're just my friend."

"You're drunk." They met eyes.

Coherency dawned. "Mallory's friend, Jane's, her's." He didn't find the name in time.

"*Chloe*, and we're missing her play because of you."

"What are you?"

"I'm trying to be a good friend, Cecil, but you're pushing it."

"What am I?"

Kindling caught in Pierre's limbs again, climbing to his heart. "Just shut up and come on."

"Scarecrow." He rubbed what body he could, his chest, his arms, his face. "Sticks and shit. You drew it on, all of you."

The last attempt, a plea. "You're our friend, Cecil."

"Nothing. Whatever you make me."

And he caught fire. "Y'know, fine, fucking *fine*. If you won't talk, I have somewhere to be. Because I'm a good friend, Cecil. A good friend."

Pierre started back through the forest, pressing its damp leaves to his heels. He knew leaving him alone there was dangerous, but nothing, he reasoned, could scrape him from the overhang, drag him where he needed to be, take him from the lake. Maybe he could've done more, but promises had to be maintained, and in any case, high emotion took precedence over whatever else he might have said or done if he had stayed longer. And it wasn't his fault anyway, and he was pulled from the others by his friendly responsibility, his generosity, to deal with this to begin with. Whatever was wrong could wait a few hours, or it could wait until morning, and everyone would come together and resolve it, whatever 'it' was. So as Mallory and Jane forgot Cecil, sitting in their seats, Pierre forgot him as he exited the forest, crossed the street, and followed the sidewalk.

At the lake, the boat still whirred. Cecil turned his head to the sound, using a root as a headrest. He recognized an echo of a voice, then another. They were all nameless, faceless friends from high school, all those people suspended above the lake, the night, drinking on the surface of oblivion.

The last chance to join them presented itself, and Cecil relapsed. He leaned toward the sounds, the lights, closer, clawing through the dirt, tumbling three feet and slapping the water above the pit, flailing at the surface, scrabbling to escape. Jane would find him hours later and bring him back to her apartment for rehabilitation.

15

THEY GRADUATED THREE HOURS ago, and Cecil stood thirteen floors above the town. No more routine, he thought, and no more bumping into each other in the hall. He would live here now. The apartment was a block away, and from his roost on a derelict parking garage, he could see a light in one his new home's windows stutter and stop, dark. The rent was cheap, and that was all he let himself know.

But they graduated, and Steve brought him to this party. Behind Cecil were a few dozen teens, graduates and underclassmen, and others filtered through the floors below them. Someone brought glow sticks which in the first hour were worn, cracked, and littered as broken bones and fading, neon blood. A group of them brought drinks, and beer cases built a short pyramid in the corner. Someone else brought the speaker, and sometimes, someone pissed all the way to the street. Someone had done it next to Cecil.

He wondered why he brought himself, or why Steve asked him to come. He had been fading from Clearwater for months, and he was only dimly a part of his old friends, a mascot of antiquity, so that nobody talked to him, and he refrained from socializing. But they would all be gone soon (he was graduating; he would be gone), and someone already left. She wasn't there tonight, at least not to Cecil's knowledge, though he spent most of the party leaning against the parapet and watching the town converge somewhere on the horizon. She was somewhere out there among the thousand beads of light slipping from windows, walking through the murky world where lights failed. And the sky above was its own town with billions of eyes scanning, watching, focusing on the boy on the roof, and the moon turned its sallow face, and a breeze pried his jacket open. No, she wouldn't be there. She wasn't in the "in" crowd.

He should be with the others, but where were they, Jane and Mallory and the other two, and how could he still lose their names? They kept him. They set his name immemorial with their own, and he couldn't be bothered even with remembering. His link to them was gone, she who lived somewhere in this sea of light and sticks, and with her absence, the others would forget him too. Maybe they already had. Maybe they left to stand now in the aftermath of two fallouts. Radiation spilled from plastic cups around him, and where had they gone after the ceremony, after the finale, after the circumstances of their friendship? They were off somewhere; they had forgotten. Cecil returned to the horror movie that brought them together, recalling all their faces but little of what they wore and none of their last names. And in every frozen recollection was Sylvia, clearer and larger than the others, glowing even, laughing this moment, punching his arm the next. But always after these scenes resurfaced, she would stare at Cecil in the theater and, ripping through months, the boy at the top of a parking garage. She stared at him now, neither frowning nor smiling, only watching him from her seat, and he shuddered. She was behind him now. She was poison, and he coughed.

"Cecil?" Some other girl. "Is that you?"

The speaker drowned everything but his name, and when he turned, the girl was unrecognizable: a crop top and curly hair.

"It's Rachel. From middle school?"

Maybe he jettisoned her with the others. She was new, a freshman, or she was so notable that a crowd insulated her, that she was someone beyond him. His absent voice agreed. "Rachel."

"How have you been?" and "It's been so long!"

A row of pins held the hair above her right ear, and Cecil saw something of the other girl. "Good. You?"

"Pretty good." She bumped his shoulder, another vestige, and he flinched, and his left side wanted to escape, to cleave from the mark she left. "Y'know," she continued, "part of me didn't think you'd graduate. Do you know what you're studying next year?"

He didn't know anything. He couldn't know anything as long as those pins tucked her hair, as long as her jaw curved the same, as long as her outline traced her. What was he studying? But why was the world converging at a single point on Rachel's face just below the eye? "I haven't thought about it. Are you…" he started without a question. He couldn't remove himself from the spot, couldn't look at the eyes or she would recur like a hammer on a splitting nail.

"Maybe drama," she said. "Maybe French."

Cecil desperately asked himself which one liked drama. Maybe Jane—she seemed the Broadway type—or Pierre, a good lead. Just keep thinking, he told himself, think anything away from her. But he should've already known who liked drama, but he shouldn't lapse back into her. Here was Jane singing, there stood Pierre on stage, but nothing matched, nothing reconciled. So he asked Rachel where she was going to college, and she said something about Vancouver.

But he didn't want to forget her. He never wanted to forget, because in forgetting, cherished fragments were guttered with the waste, and no choice was given for which tokens sank or floated in submarine, cerebral pools. He wanted only to sanitize his history, to blanket everything with the reassurance that it was past and never present, lording only embarrassment over him and nothing greater. Or he wanted to stop talking to Rachel, to stop the music pulsing in his feet, to pull from the cold, concrete wall he leaned against, to fall in open air above the town, to fall like a dream, like a character of campfire dramas and fifth-grade folktales.

"Are you doing okay?"

But she spoke to someone else somewhere else, someone in his place but not his person. He had already decided to fall and stood now as a corpse with a pulse in his feet. A sheet of light covered the town below, the town far off, the town full of permanent people, people who would never submit to history. And between this and the open sky—the sky collapsed with stars like raindrops on a sidewalk—was a cool breeze again, and Cecil started pulling himself to the ledge, and Rachel saw what was happening, couldn't comprehend what was happening, and hurried away to find someone more qualified.

He looked into the sky, and before he could move further, a text came.

*Wanna hang?* Jane said. *We're all going to the lake.*

He sighed; he breathed; he laughed at himself. He waited two minutes to respond, not thinking but watching the air, breathing. *Could you pick me up?*

*For sure. Where at?*

He told her.

*Be there in 5.*

He withdrew from the ledge, landed back on the cement roof. He left before Rachel could return, down a flight of stairs and a weathered elevator with an arabesque sliding door. The parking garage fell away behind him, and the world held solid. He could hardly hear the party from the street.

Cecil had walked or driven with others down this street more than he cared to recount and for many more reasons that he wished to stow away, vices always near the surface. He waited at the foot of the garage. To his left lived liquor stores and bars that didn't ask for ID, warehouses, and friends with cars who could take him anywhere, do anything. And to the right was the lake, and here an SUV came down the street, slowing, stopping. The windows were down, and Jane waved him inside.

"Hey, champ," she said as he climbed in. "What are you doing down here?"

She pulled a U-turn and hadn't heard the music from the thirteenth floor, but Cecil couldn't find an excuse. "Just walking."

"Do you live here?"

"No, I don't." He fooled himself. "Do you?"

She shook her head and started back where she came. The car inside was black leather and smelled of nothing or autumn. It was too clean, and Cecil reasoned it was her parents' car, but something opposed its store-bought purity: a trinket of a painting hung from her rearview mirror. It rocked in the wind but was easy to parse. Two figures stood on a boat, altogether a few dots, perhaps another boat to their left, perhaps debris. A gray lake was dashed around them, and a permanent, orange sun centered the piece, its reflection a residue on the water. If he paid more attention in art class, he maybe could have named the artist.

"What's the painting?" he asked, breaking a silence he hadn't noticed.

"Not sure. Something by Monet." She tried a French accent, scuffed it, and laughed. "Do you like it?"

"Yeah." But he couldn't pull himself from the sun, and when he could, he was one of the boatmen watching it. The composition swirled and centered around that eye like a drain, like a portal. It threw Cecil out of himself until Jane asked, "So you were just walking around down here?"

He turned to her, and she flicked her attention from him to the road. Was she concerned? Cecil saw in her something he had only seen before in Sylvia (how she lost her power here in the car, here with Jane) when they met. Jane was curious.

But still he deflected. "Late night."

"It's only ten." She smirked, and he was suddenly compelled to answer in full, to say why he was there and cut himself open; to pour everything he thought, everything he ever thought and did, to her; to expound the greatest toils of himself, how he broke against the waves, battered, beaten, sewed together again. He was sporadic; he was stuck in the whims of his body, if it wanted drink or cheap fun or empty fun, and as he lay in bed after nights like these, he would learn and relearn that he would do everything he never wanted, everything he needed. He was compelled to tell Jane how much he needed her and the others and no one else or himself. Was it her nature to reveal these things, or was he starved, too ready to answer?

But only a drop broke from the flood. "There was a party," he said, "for graduation. Not great, though." Jane sped through a yellow light and nodded, wind whipping her hair around the cabin. He wanted to say more but didn't know how, and then he remembered. "Were you the one who liked musicals?"

She bobbed her shoulders as if weighing something. "Here and there. Did you want to get into it?"

He didn't. "Maybe."

"You should talk to Chloe. She's deep in that shit."

The actor.

"Not that it's shit," she stumbled, "just like, y'know."

"Yeah." But who was Jane if not the actor? He asked her what she enjoyed.

"I mean, I hang out a lot." A sigh drifted from her nose. When Jane lay awake at night thinking about how everything could have gone differently—how she could've talked to Sylvia before the divide, talked to Chloe any more than she had in middle school, in high school, the impact a single intrusion could impart on one life—on those nights, she would also think how little she was invested in. She had friends, but nothing of herself, a patchwork doll of attempts: a mediocre pianist, a sentimental poet, a cook with a gaunt book of recipes. Even now in the back seat, a camera hid in its bag, the trinket of a dwindling photographer. She hoped Cecil hadn't seen it. "I get out a lot. Do you like it down here?"

He shifted in his seat. "It's alright."

"You wouldn't recommend?"

They were out of that part of town and turning onto a road parallel to the forest. Houses morphed from their tight, wedged apartments to dispersed, country things, suburban vignettes. They passed a neighborhood, maybe two, and a yellow sign stamped with a jumping deer caught the headlights, and the wind caught her question. She let it rest, and they sat in silence, watching the world blur.

Cecil broke it. "So whose place are we going to?"

She smirked again. "God's, I guess, if you're into that."

"Um."

"Glass Lake," she said. "Going swimming."

"Isn't it, like—" he stuck a hand out the window and felt the wind erode its sense. "Cold?"

"Blankets in the trunk, if you need them."

"I don't have my suit, either." He carried nothing but his phone and a thin wallet.

She laughed. "Bro, that's the point. We're going skinny dipping."

The old friends had done it before. He joined them once, but he could never repeat it as the group grew in number and substances, informal and impolite. And the novelty wasn't something he was fond of. Despite any madcap party habits, stripping degraded, and on the nights he drank on shore or in the boat, he felt equally degraded in watching, but avoiding people altogether would brand him an outcast. Were these present friends following the old group's games? And would he go with them, comfortable or complacent?

"Innocent fun. You totally don't have to if you don't want to."

"No, I'm down." Had he said it?

Jane nodded, paused, and asked, "So what makes it 'alright' back there?" She trailed off. "I just take walks sometimes and was wondering if it was worth it."

She pushed it again, and did she really care to know, or was she prying, pinning something on him, some label, something incriminating with which to claim to herself, "This is Cecil Monroe. This is below us." He gathered she didn't go on walks at all, but even in this lie and its escalations in Cecil's head, he couldn't help but feel again invited to answer. An honest curiosity lit her eyes, her posture. He reasoned now that she had seen the party thirteen stories up, and now she was something of a rescuer, a liberator. She was holy and made him feel the same.

He pushed his knees against his chest. A wedge inside still stopped his answering in full, tightness in every tendon telling him to keep steady. "It's rough."

"For you? Or for everyone?" She pulled into a neighborhood and parked against the sidewalk. Across the road was the forest, but nothing apparent marked an entrance. Mist settled in the silhouettes of oaks and elms, and the treetops swayed as one mass, a verdant wave. He had never gone to the lake with them before. Was this where they always entered?

"For everyone." They left the car, and Cecil grabbed a blanket from the back. Jane stuffed a few towels into a black backpack.

"You included?"

He was breaking. "Yeah."

"Well, if you ever want to talk." They started across the street. "I think you're cool."

He smiled for reasons which wouldn't surface.

Jane led the way inside, and the dusky canopy filled the empty spaces between trees, growing to a tangible blindness. His guide flicked a flashlight to life, projecting a shallow spray of yellow light. These woods looked alien to Cecil, all knotted brush and protruding limbs, reaching branches needing to be shoved, flinging back after he passed. And nothing held a shadow against the flashlight. Surfaces of near logs and their mosses and mushrooms were revealed with brilliant clarity, starker than anything he had seen before. When had he last wandered in these woods, stepped off the boat and lost himself in this space?

A minute passed without speaking, then two, then conversation hushed ahead. The flashlight spray found a clearing, and the two travelers stepped onto the wooded shore of the lake. From what Cecil could tell, it was a small beach, or not a beach at all, but a strip of soil and rock declining into the lake. When the light hit two boys in the water, Jane turned it off.

"Look who I found," she crooned to them. Jane grabbed his arm and brought him outside the tree line. The moon highlighted everything in slim, silver outlines, and he saw the upper halves of Mallory and Pierre in the shallows.

Someone asked, "Who?"

"Hey." He revealed himself and felt he shouldn't be there, that he didn't have the license to join this group under these circumstances. He was invading something they had grown together and without him, and he was awkward to their friendship, and his blood froze as Jane began to strip next to him. But when he spoke, Pierre gave a quiet cheer, and some reprieve lived in that. Mallory was silent, and Cecil forgot who he was, forgot how he thought of him.

"Snacks are in the boat," Pierre called as Jane waded in to join them. And why were they so comfortable together? Was this some initiation? He put the thought outside. From his brief experience with Jane, he assumed she wouldn't allow any hazing. But the thought returned at intervals through the night that he was missing something important, had missed something important, that he lived in the consequence of failed recognition.

His eye caught on the boat, a wooden shell buried half in the dirt, tombed in roots. Somewhere across the lake, somewhere his eyes might only glean on the horizon if the sun was out, was the town's official boat landing, the dock he always cast from with the others—old ghosts now, it seemed. But here was a paltry place, unkempt earth, an abandoned raft, and a rotting dock of loose boards, and who sat at its end? A naked back with blond, lampshade hair hunched small and pale against the moon, and it must be Chloe, yes, the theater girl.

The others stole whispering glances at her from the shallows.

In the boat's hull were propped an opened case of soda and a bulky carton of colored crackers. He grabbed a handful of these and returned to the group. This was the last chance to swim with the others—stripping anytime after would reveal his discomfort. But as he neared the conversation and saw only their heads above water, he couldn't do it, and he took refuge between tree roots, draping Jane's blanket over his shoulders. A few yards away, she nodded to him, acknowledged him.

"Is it that you don't want to talk to her?" Pierre was asking.

"I don't know. I don't know." Mallory looked past him to the girl on the dock. "Not like this."

Pierre sighed. "Is it the naked part?"

"Obviously it's the naked part, Pierre," Jane snapped.

"I don't know," he said, "maybe he's into it."

A pause. Mallory spoke as if reluctant of his words. "I just want to talk to her more. I think she wants to too." He looked at her, looked back. She held her head now. "I think."

Every crunch of food rattled through Cecil's skull, and he became aware that in the dialogue's pauses, the others may have heard him eating, listening. He eavesdropped, but with how little he knew of them, he could add nothing. A group of bats struggled in the air to their right, and Cecil tried to distract his attention to them.

"Is she okay?" Mallory asked. "Have you guys talked to her today?"

They both denied it. "But I'll go get her," Jane said.

"Thank you."

She sloshed down the shallows.

"Has she not told you *anything*?" Pierre asked.

Jane sat next to the girl on the dock now, and the bats found their places in the canopy. Cecil had no choice now but to listen. A silent space followed Pierre's inquiry, and Cecil forced himself to stop eating until the silence resolved.

"You don't have to say anything if you don't want."

"Her mom. It's been hitting her hard lately," Mallory said. "It was like this at graduation too."

"So you've talked to her about it?"

"Yeah."

Some words caught wind from the dock, but nothing comprehensible. Pierre nodded. "That's all a friend can do."

"I guess. But talking doesn't do much."

"Have you talked a lot today?"

"A little. I just wanted her to enjoy it, you know?" He slipped his head underwater and continued when he resurfaced, pulling strings of hair from his face. "She told me—please don't tell anyone about this."

"Of course."

"She told me she's been seeing things. That she saw something today in the auditorium seats. But she won't say what's up."

Cecil watched each pod of two and figured Mallory had a thing for Chloe. He warmed to the former of these two now that he exposed weakness, now that he was more than Sylvia's ex and someone of little importance at prom, the longest stretch of time he and Cecil had shared together. Chloe was still a bundle of secrets, though Mallory needled a hole in her side, and everything started to unravel. He would know her soon.

The actor. The hallucinator. The girl who lost half of everything and dangled her feet in the water under a full moon.

# 16

THE BOYS WERE AT the bar an hour before the show. Nobody wanted to get drunk, but Pierre wanted to go, and Mallory rarely went anywhere without him. Cecil joined against his discretion, and now that he was here, his thoughts turned on themselves, rolled with unreal logic.

A pile of thoughts had built itself into a corner of his brain like an old scarecrow, like a clot of dead birds beside it. Its base was Sylvia, and above it rose a smattering of loose ebony, molting feathers: disparate, dividing hemispheres of Cecil and his friends. (His friends! he called them now. He had woven into them well, but still something else lingered, something that could never be reconciled with another person. Perfect trust was gone.) At the top of the corpses was a crow still alive and bleeding, the memory of a woman falling stale from his car, and the bird rang as an alarm against his skull, battered its uninjured wing against his hull, and shook the cup in his hand. The crow only perched yesterday. Those minutes still played vividly on the reel. "You're nobody," she said. "Just their friend."

"Talk to me," Cecil said through alcohol's fog. Mallory and Pierre held a conversation with each other, but Cecil couldn't hear them, and now they turned in the booth to face him, Mallory to his left, Pierre across the table. There were a hundred Mallorys and a hundred Pierres, each layered atop each other, and when they moved, some layers persisted a moment in place.

"You good?" Pierre asked.

"There's a lot to talk about me," he pleaded.

But it all came out together, and Mallory glanced sideways at Pierre, whispering, "'There's... lot...?'"

"He's done, right? Glass is empty?"

"Yeah."

"Good."

They resumed. Cecil deduced they were talking about Chloe, and he wanted above everything so that the desire was no less than necessity to join the conversation, to leave himself, Cecil Monroe, in the caves of his body, his thoughts, his vision. But still the bird chanted on its flock, crippling Cecil over the table, contracting. "She's a bitch," he said.

Silence in the group, but the rest of the bar still hummed. Mallory shrunk into the wall, and Pierre gave an empty "What?"

"Talk to me."

"Are you alright?" Pierre whispered.

He spoke so quietly it may have been a mistake. "Who am I?"

"Cecil?" Mallory said.

He rubbed bleary hands to his eyes. "What?"

"What's wrong?"

"I'm nobody."

Mallory and Pierre met covert eyes again. The latter asked if Cecil wanted to talk about this outside.

And the bird atop the pile diffused to shrieks and feathers, a black backdrop on which the woman stood, the woman lay, the woman bled. "You're nothing," she echoed against the alley, and he mirrored aloud. "Nothing."

Mallory nodded, another silent exchange. "We should go," Pierre said, placing a hand near Cecil.

But none of it could be blamed on him, or everything could be blamed on him, but in any case, she had brought him here, and she wouldn't leave. Again she was recognized, again the chains broke in Cecil's mind, again she was revealed in full, terrifying history: she who made senior year perfect, she whom he chased in these new friends, she whom he dredged for. It was love, it was reason, it was an answer to all the questions he never knew to ask. But she was gone, and he sat now as a collage of uncertainty, of jittering in the bar, stranded on a solitary isle in some recess of the psyche. But these friends, the boys beside him, the girls at some theater, lifted him from the sandbar and back into the life Sylvia gave him, the life of Cecil Monroe.

But the name fell apart when he held it too long, and at times he reverted to someone nameless, someone accustomed. He was this boy now.

"Her fault," he said, leaning forward again, wiping his eyes again.

Mallory said, "Chloe?"

Or maybe it was their fault, these friends who brought him to himself. This was hope: they told him they were glad to have him, but when they left, he turned hollow, Cecil Monroe in name alone, nothing interesting, nothing to do. They seduced him. Or maybe this insipid Cecil was the genuine exhibit, and all the mental chiropractics they performed only brought him further from himself and into empty hope for a life that was never his.

He cupped his temples in his palms. "You lied to me."

"I'm sorry?" Pierre said. Mallory pressed himself in the corner of the booth, mute.

He choked. "You never loved me."

"What? Cecil."

"I'm my own *person*."

"We appreciate you hanging with us. Really." He tried to de-escalate the fervor in his voice, but to Cecil, birds stacked higher on the pile.

"Be my friend." He cradled his stomach. "Just leave me alone."

"I—" Mallory stammered, warming back to life. "Cecil?"

But Mallory was the worst of it: the soft kid, the accomplice. He had no purpose but to drive Cecil further in the ruse. He never talked to him, only watched him scramble, and he harbored glee at witnessing a man reduced, a boy diminished. Mallory could've saved him from it all if he hadn't dated Sylvia, if he hadn't brought Sylvia into their group.

This would be the end of it.

Pierre stood, reaching for Cecil's arm, but in the same moment, Cecil grabbed his empty glass and swung blind to the right. It found its mark, slamming against a sponge of skin, and when he turned to preview the damage, Mallory had curled in a ball and bandaged his cheek with overlapped hands. Soft weeping came over him, out from the folds of his fingers, and the same grief mirrored in Cecil. He started to cry. He started to think. If given the chance, he may have apologized and awakened back into sobriety, but Pierre ripped him from the table. He fell to the floor. Pierre offered his hand, but Cecil clambered to his feet and ran through the bar, through the door, going nowhere.

A QUEEN STOOD IN layers of pale makeup and jewelry. Her attendant waited beside and nervously informed her and the audience, "She speaks much of her father, says she hears there's tricks in the world, and beats her heart."

A second man stood to the side, but Mallory couldn't look at him anymore. He recognized him from high school, and any remembrance ignited Cecil, and once he was reinstated in Mallory's mind, he would not leave. But Mallory had a habit now to forget: he scratched his right arm. No logical link connected forgetting and scratching, but the routine brought his mind away from everything, and now his arm was painted a deep red, and a concentrated streak at the forearm held taut like pulled rubber.

But the ghosts were never gone for long, and when Cecil lapsed in Mallory's attention, his parents' silhouettes took his cataclysmic role. And when they left at last, there were always doubts—doubts of Chloe's love, of the depths of his friendships (did he and Jane really grow that night, or was it only circumstance that joined them for a moment, circumstance that would change the next day?), doubts of himself as a friend, a lover, a solitary soul. He was too small, and a breeze careened through the audience, eating at his skin, and a court of ghosts hung always above him, always higher than he could see, draping memories like guns and guillotines and tarot cards at the edge of his sight.

"Where is the beauteous Majesty of Denmark?"

She spoke and was there, stumbling in from the side, wincing as the light hit her face. Her dress frayed at the sleeves and hems and tore in ribbons around her legs, and sackcloth mended the gaps. She became a creature of growing squalor. Her hair was likewise torn and strewn in chunks, though sections remembered the folds of a crown. She was almost a spirit, but it was makeup, Mallory reasoned, it was makeup and nothing more. Her eyes flew around the theater, searching, searching, and landing for only a second at Mallory and Jane, their seats, their corner of the crowd. And again she appeared to break. Her shoulders shrugged and her lips parted and trembled. Her eyes dug into those rows, excavating, exhuming, pulling nothing from the well. Mallory didn't even know if she saw him, but in that second, he saw more of her than he ever had before. She was a tenuous girl, a girl of strings. But in the same breath, she returned to the play and wouldn't look again at Mallory or that corner of the room.

The queen said, "How now, Ophelia?"

She sang something on fragile air and bobbed across the stage, and though he couldn't decipher the words, she was beautiful.

"Alas sweet lady," said the queen, "what imports this song?"

A pause. Did she forget it? But she faced the crowd and gazed somewhere distant. "He is dead and gone, lady." Two lines of tears dragged her cheeks. Her body clenched stiff. "He is dead and gone."

In those Friday nights together, those nights when Chloe would act a few lines to appease Mallory's curiosity, she never cried. He believed this was the thrill of performance, the added effects of a real performance, but he only believed as far as the belief's distraction held. Something deeper than the play tortured her, Mallory knew, Mallory was sure, but he couldn't think about it now. He would bring it up later, bring it up after the play, after dead men and meathooks and sleeping pills, all ghosts in the system, left the rafters. No, it wasn't just acting, it couldn't be acting. Something of Chloe's own life rotted, and he would ask her about it when the curtains closed, when he would ask her if they could make things official. He had to be happy now, or negligent. He itched his arm.

She said, "And will he not come again?"

How much longer could he endure in the audience? He thought to ask Jane how long the show had left, but he couldn't bring himself into the world. Was this how Chloe felt, claustrophobic in a world so distant?

"And will he not come again?" she repeated, lilting a fragile song. "No, no, he is dead. Go to thy deathbed. He will never come again."

She didn't look like herself anymore, turning closer to her character. He doubted if she was ever Chloe Barnett or always Ophelia, always a friend, a daughter, only a list of titles and their obligations. She was never more to Mallory than friend and lover, and neither was he anything more to her. Two could never share themselves. Any bond between them was founded and built upon appearances of the self, never the self entire, so he could never really love her, even as he comforted himself in her image. She would only exist in part; he in part. She could never love him either, nor could Jane, Pierre, Cecil.

The name again burned the bruise, and he brought a hand to it. But the same hand recoiled to itch, to forget, manic fingers withdrawing to the streaks scrawled in his forearm. Every scrape was dynamite in the skin, but it relaxed, it soothed. Habit suffocated thought.

Chloe left the stage for a time. Another hour passed, and Mallory still dug. Jane had left most of the popcorn for him and placed the bag in his lap, falling limp against his arm, but the play was ending now. A poisoned murder closed the curtains, and to Mallory's dismay, they didn't reopen for applause. It was over. Lights warmed alive. Life resumed. Now he could find her.

"Wow," Jane said. "That was awesome. How—" she turned to Mallory and flinched. "Holy shit, you're bleeding."

His eyes darted from her to the door. "It's alright, I'll fix it." He struggled to speak and ripped his feet forward, weaving through the crowd before she could respond. Pierre stood here at the back of the audience and tried to catch Mallory as he ran, but he was outside in the same moment. Jane found Pierre looking into the foyer, following the trail outside.

"What's the hurry for?" he asked.

"He was bleeding. Went to clean up."

But the bathroom was to their right. Pierre didn't mention it.

"What happened with Cecil?"

He shrugged. "Just got drunk. Lost himself for now."

She pressed further below her breath. "I mean what did he do, what did he say? Where is he now?"

"He called Chloe a bitch and hit Mallory—"

"Mal told me," she interrupted. "Is he safe?"

He breathed deep. "Yeah. He's at the lake."

Jane remembered to forget responsibility until tomorrow. She and Cecil and Mallory could work everything out together then. Tonight was a celebration, even if a friend slept in the woods. "Alright," she decided. "Alright. He knows his way out."

"I should've stayed with him." His face lowered.

"Was it bad?"

"Real bad." He shook his head again, looking back outside. "I should've stayed."

She put an arm on his shoulder. "I'll talk to him. Okay?"
A hollow nod.

Mallory turned the corner of the Vintage and scaled the fire escape on its side. It was midnight in the town, and a breeze chilled his skin. Stars hung between rungs in the climb, and the moon loomed closer than it ever had, a lump of gray light. On the roof, wind whistled and stung the open patch on his arm. She wasn't there yet. He looked over the side, watching the audience ripple from the theater, and there went Jane, Pierre following.

His heart rapped against its wires. Had Chloe forgotten their meeting, and would she appear in that crowd somewhere? Or did she remember and purposefully avoid him? He waited for the traffic to end before thinking of giving up. She hadn't texted him, and neither had Pierre or Jane or—

A metal door groaned open behind him, and she walked eternally under the moon. She wore gym shorts, a sweatshirt, and the sun hat, and as she neared, the carvings on his arm became apparent, and she hurried to him, smoothing the flesh with a finger. "What happened, are you okay?"

"Hey," he said. "Um." He nodded. Their eyes met, and she was a warm, holy thing, but even now he could only see the character, Ophelia's dread but Chloe's all the same. Something was wrong, or everything was wrong.

She pressed too hard on the product of his habit, and his legs shook for an instant, his legs shook and he lost composure. Maybe she didn't see it. But now her eyebrows furrowed, now she spoke with cautious sincerity, a voice like a warning. "Mallory?"

"Yeah?"

"What happened?"

"You were wonderful tonight." He hurried.

"Why is your arm bleeding?"

"I love you." And it was done in part. A wave overcame his senses, and when it relinquished to the sea, nothing lingered. No thoughts plagued him, nothing of his parents or Cecil or anyone or anywhere but Ophelia and the backdrop of the moon.

She blinked. "I love you too, but you're hurt."

But he couldn't tell her he did it. He wanted to, but something immovable blocked the connection, blocked all connections, so that lies were forced as to who he really was, just as Chloe lied, Cecil lied, Pierre and Jane lied, always approximating themselves. "It was Cecil. He was just messing around. It's nothing."

"Oh." She drifted. "Is he okay then?"

"He's fine."

"Mallory, this looks like it really hurts."

He blurted, "Is something wrong?"

She started, froze. He never saw her stutter. "Nothing's wrong. I love you."

"And you had fun tonight? Did well?"

She pursed her lips and nodded. The air hollowed as the doors closed behind the last of the audience taking the street. If Mallory looked over the side again, he would see Jane walking by, headed for the Long Reel where she would buy two tickets for a new movie and wait in the foyer for Chloe. Presently, Chloe looked past Mallory, and he followed her gaze to the forest or somewhere deep inside. She was thinking or relaxing, and Mallory stared with her, trying to find parallel peace.

"We just can't be together right now."

Everything that the tide had swallowed resurfaced, beached, and terrorized his breath and the gossamer bond between them. He whispered, "Chlo?"

"I mean, we can be. But you know how Henry is." She sighed. "I don't want it either, but it isn't about me." She shivered against the wind, against herself, uncontrollably, as if coming undone.

"It's about Henry?"

"It's about Phoebe." She barreled her eyes closed, pressed out latent images. "She needs me to do well. And Henry needs her who needs me."

"I need you too."

"I know." She hugged him, and the hat's brim covered his head. "I need you too, too. It just has to wait a while."

"You're so cold."

"We'll be okay. We've always been okay." She kissed his cheek, noticed the welt, and stood apart again. "Mallory?" She was wary of the ground she crossed. "What really happened tonight?"

But Mallory again was cornered. Only now did he realize the scope of his detriment to her private life. He soured the relationship of father and daughter, providing a fixed point to argue over, never to agree on until now, two years too late. And is this what Phoebe would have wanted? She had never met him, and any chance she had was in elementary school, and he had changed irrevocably since then, he thought. Now Henry used Phoebe's imagined will to tear them apart, that much was clear, corroding Chloe until she agreed. Mallory knew it was corrupt, but was he himself wrong for usurping their personal lives? By Henry's argument, he was now associated with the dead mother, and every time she and Chloe were together, she would have been reminded of Phoebe, the day she left, and the empty note. In loving her, he became a memento.

He understood himself now as the cause of Chloe's paranormal life. She confided in him twice now, at graduation and as they relaxed here above the Vintage two months ago, how Phoebe's ghost appeared to her at random. Was his presence in her life provoking these encounters, or at least stoking her grief with increased memory? Chloe told him the first time she saw Phoebe was at the lake the day she died, the day she met him. He would forever be branded. He would always represent the unrepresentable, the shadows at the bottom of a lake, the eidolon of memory, and her chronic, paralyzing past. He would never be more than remembered.

"Mallory?"

But he was running from the roof, down the stairs, disappearing.

"Mal," she called. "Come back, please, it's okay."

He couldn't hear her over the wind, over himself.

# 17

MALLORY RAN IN HIS own place in time across the road, ran for some time and found the trail to the woods. He remembered the house party the night prior and, on remembering, sought to expunge it from the past. They could never love him or anyone in full, not for lack of effort, but for grief's bedrock under every conversation.

As he trampled into the black canopy, he traced his thoughts through everything he remembered with the others. He turned his somber wrath on anything remembered as guilty of an unknown crime, censoring them all: the days of elementary school to high school's close all dotted with Pierre and Chloe and Sylvia, and had he forgotten her already? Eight years together, and one apart had overturned Sylvia's permanence? And had only a minute undone Chloe? He realized at this censoring's end that nothing cohesive sustained him. Of his twenty-one years, only thin seconds remained of a pure Mallory. Every moment was shared with another.

Something rustled in the trees to his left. Mallory jolted his head at the sound, and a pair of blue eyes glanced back. They were human and scared, but he couldn't address them. He needed to leave. And in the same breath the eyes appeared, they turned away, and the figure stumbled back through the forest.

He was no one anymore. Denying himself company, he no longer lived as the reflection of others. He drifted on a past of radio static, a vacant sea. Mallory tightened his muscles against the cold and the dark, and the trees broke now on familiar ground. Before him, the short shore of dirt and roots broke the tide's grasp. The old boat slept against a tree growing offshore, and another memory of Chloe surfaced which Mallory cast back. The moon's reflection cracked against the water, and quiet dusk pervaded the shore. Only fireflies and crickets pierced the idyll.

He would do it now or wish he'd done it. He waded to the skiff and pushed into deeper waters, imagining no trouble stirred here, nothing that would turn his mind to its bottom. His eyes turned up, and there was the moon again with its stars, the eye of the dead and all its single spies. Ink swirled around the boat, and he grabbed an oar and animated it with all the emotion of the day, the life, slamming it into the floor, cracking a hole wide enough to bleed black water. The boat drifted to the heart of the lake, and the wind roared. Mallory lay in the hull, a shield from the weather, and cried.

He could feel it coming as Glass Lake grew in the boat, in his clothes and skin, cold. A greater sense clawed at his limbs, tore at his brain, and let his heart quiet. Just a moment of courage, and every flashback and recollection and memoir would be gone, forgotten, and he would be wholly Mallory, a boy unto himself, not the product of manifold days passing as bad dreams.

The moon was beautiful and terrible and diagnostic. Maybe it always was. The boat filled, sunk, and the lake swallowed the empty space.

9 798218 314644